Katie's heart thumped so hard, she thought for sure it would burst free.

Spending time with Ward might not be one of the wisest decisions she'd ever made. Especially with the twinkle in his eyes when he glanced her way.

"Would you enjoy an ice cream?" Ward put his large hand over hers.

Her skin tingled. "Yes. I can't remember the last time I enjoyed such a treat."

Ward helped her navigate the busy street, leading her through the horses, buggies and the occasional automobile as if he had a sixth sense.

Why wasn't she better at the art of flirtation? Unless he asked her a question that required a direct answer, her tongue remained glued to the roof of her mouth. The only good thing about being unable to speak was that she wouldn't be able to say anything incriminating.

"Here you go." Ward handed her a cone filled with a scoop of vanilla ice cream. "There's a small park around the corner. Would you feel safe sitting there?"

She glanced up at him. "Of course. Anyone would feel safe with you."

Books by Cynthia Hickey

Love Inspired Heartsong Presents

Cooking Up Love
Taming the Sheriff
An Unconventional Lady
In a Texas Ranger's Arms

CYNTHIA HICKEY

Multipublished author Cynthia Hickey is represented by the MacGregor Literary Agency. Her first novel, a cozy mystery, was released in 2007, and she hasn't stopped publishing since. Writing is like breathing for her. Cynthia lives in Arizona with her husband, one of their seven children, two dogs, two cats and a fish named Floyd. She has five grandchildren, who keep her busy and tell everyone they know that "Nana is a writer." Visit her website at www.cynthiahickey.com.

CYNTHIA HICKEY

In a Texas Ranger's Arms

HEARTSONG
PRESENTS

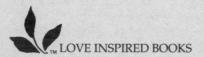 ^{TM} LOVE INSPIRED BOOKS

Recycling programs for this product may not exist in your area.

ISBN-13: 978-0-373-48717-2

IN A TEXAS RANGER'S ARMS

Copyright © 2014 by Cynthia M. Hickey

www.Harlequin.com

Printed in U.S.A.

So we can say for sure, "The Lord is my Helper.
I am not afraid of anything man can do to me."
—*Hebrews* 13:6

Acknowledgments

Thank you to all the fans who adore the Harvey Girls as much as I do. To my family for their constant support. To God for allowing me to write these books.

Chapter 1

1910

Katie Gamble cast one last glance over her shoulder. No Amos Moore.

With a grin, she clutched the handle of her satchel and stepped onto the train that would take her to her new home and job in Somerville, Texas. As she moved down the aisle, she found a seat next to a petite blonde with the bluest eyes Katie had ever seen.

"Howdy. I'm Sarah Chapman, and I'm a Harvey Girl." Her eyes twinkled.

"Hello, I'm Katie." She stashed her bag in an overhead compartment. The papers in the hidden pocket on her slip crinkled as she stretched to place the bag overhead. She peered at her companion. Had she heard? Although the papers were hidden, she still wasn't eager to let her other belongings out of sight, even if it was the land deed that mattered the most. She didn't want to answer any questions either. However, she need not have worried, because the girl continued to chatter to anyone willing to listen.

"You can have the window seat, if you'd like, Katie. The motion outside the window makes my stomach roll. Why did you sign on with the Harvey Company?" Sarah smoothed the skirt of her green dress. "I'm going to find a husband. As the youngest of eleven children, there isn't much left for me back home in Missouri, and there are a lot of men along the railroad line."

A husband? Katie hadn't really thought of that. Maybe once Amos stopped chasing her, she could think about settling down and having a family of her own. "I joined up so I don't have to worry about where my next meal is coming from or how I'm going to put a roof over my head."

"You poor thing. You sound like you've had a rough time." A statuesque brunette reached across Sarah and patted Katie's hand. "I'm Rachel Warren, and while I am searching for a taste of independence, I won't turn down the right man if he asks for my hand. After all, the Harvey women are bringing refinement to towns desperately in need of morally upright women." She glanced around the car. "Looks like we're the only three heading to the Santa Fe."

Refinement? That left Katie out. Was it wrong in God's eyes to steal back something that had been stolen from her? She didn't know. But she would keep it pinned to her underskirts until the day she died, if need be. The deed and the document showing that oil had been discovered on her family's land was one secret she had to keep to herself. She sat down on the upholstered seat, the cushion letting out a soft whoosh of air.

Katie leaned her elbow on the windowsill as the train pulled away from the platform with a jolt. She rested her chin in the cup of her hand, and watched the prairie speed past. Guilt over her actions warred with the idea she had done nothing wrong. Sure, the land was hers, but maybe she shouldn't have taken the few coins left on Amos's dresser. When the man had returned to his room after his nightly visit to the bar, had he yelled? Punched the wall? Hit someone? She didn't know, but she knew he'd come looking for her. He would never let go of her family's property so easily.

She tuned out the friendly chatter of her companions and touched her chin, all too familiar with the consequences of his anger. She blinked back stinging tears. Once she settled into her new job, she would evaluate her feelings. If nothing else, she could pay Amos back the money. Not that the dirty scoundrel deserved it, but because she wanted to be a better person than that.

An automobile rumbled along a dirt road beside the track. What would it be like to ride in one? Would a town the size of Somerville have automobiles? After her small mountain community Somerville sounded like a bustling town.

She turned to the other girls. "Do any of y'all know anything about this town we're headed to?"

"I do." Sarah practically bounced in her seat. "It's a cotton town. There're some ranches, too, I think. My cousin once worked at the Harvey restaurant there, and she wrote to me all about it. Said sometimes the Texas Rangers come and stay at the hotel. She said they are all the most handsome men." She clasped her hands together. "I want to marry one of them!"

Rangers! There couldn't be a worse place for Katie to go. Especially after overhearing someone talking about a man in a saloon who was asking around about a girl who had stolen his deed and his money. Signing up to join the Fred Harvey Company could be the worst decision she had ever made. Instead of hiding in the wilderness, she was right on the railroad line where hundreds of people traveled.

She wiped her palms on her skirt. Keeping her secret was more imperative than ever. Mama always told her that the legal system believed the word of men over women, regardless of their reputations.

After seeing how Amos treated both of them, and got away with it, Katie was inclined to believe her mother. The man seemed to have friends in powerful places, one of them being the sheriff of Katie's hometown. Until she could prove he wasn't the man he claimed to be, she needed to find a way to support herself. The job as a Harvey Girl in Texas had sounded like just the thing. What a mistake. She leaned her head in the palm of her hand.

"I heard you aren't allowed to keep company with men unless chaperoned." Rachel used her reflection in the window to smooth her hair. "But there are always ways around the rules."

Not for Katie. If she followed the rules to the letter, she wouldn't attract any attention.

"You're awful quiet, Katie." Sarah laid a hand on her shoulder. "Not worried, are you?"

"No, just soaking in all that the two of you are saying."

"Well." Sarah plopped back. "I'm as nervous as a hen."

Rachel laughed. "With your cute face, you'll be married before the end of your contract."

"I certainly hope so." Sarah giggled.

Katie stifled a sigh. Was that all the Harvey establishment was about? A place to find a husband? Surely not. The woman who had interviewed her seemed very business-like and had admitted to remaining unmarried despite numerous proposals. It shouldn't be too hard for Katie to do the same. Men weren't always what these two girls thought they were.

The train clanked to a stop in Houston, offering the passengers a chance to straighten their legs while new ones boarded. Katie grabbed her purse and followed the other two girls down the steps.

Excited chatter assaulted her ears. Families greeted loved ones, others saw family members off. Katie sighed. She'd boarded at the last minute in order to escape Amos. No one had sent her on her way with tears and a smile. Maybe a curse or two once Amos realized she had taken what he wanted.

She turned, searching for Sarah and Rachel. Lost in her thoughts for one minute and the two chatter birds disappeared. Katie whirled to head in another direction. Her nose pressed into a solid wall of man.

Her gaze traveled from a tan shirt, up to hazel eyes, and back down to focus on a shining metal star.

"My apologies." Hitching her skirts, she turned and dashed into the depot. *Please, Lord, tell me the man isn't after me.*

After boarding the train, Ward Alston pulled his hat low over his eyes and settled down to sleep for the short ride. The wound in his side burned like nothing else, but the chatter from the bevy of beauties a few rows back soothed him. The one with hair as dark as the night had taken flight like a bird after running into him. If not for the fact her elbow had connected with his side, he would have enjoyed the contact with such a lovely lady.

As it was—not much harm done. With his mother and sisters hovering close, home would provide the rest he needed to heal.

"I got a glimpse of him," one of the women said. "He's a looker, for sure."

"He's a Ranger," another said.

"Even better."

Ward smiled under his hat. Lovelies looking for husbands. There were a few single men in Somerville, but most of them were only passing through. He wished the ladies luck. Somehow, he'd have to make sure they took him off the eligibility list. As long as he worked as a Texas Ranger, he had no plans to take a wife. He had no desire to leave behind a widow. The battle in San Benito, and the bullet graze on his rib cage, only enforced that conviction. Some of his fellow Rangers found time to marry, but the travel took a toll on their family lives. When, and if, Ward married, he wanted to be ready to settle down and not leave the wife and kids behind.

"Somerville!" The conductor roamed the cars announcing their arrival.

Taking a deep breath, Ward shoved his hat back on his head and stood to help the women get their bags down. The one who had run into him ducked her head when she claimed hers, then skedaddled like a mouse. Shy, that one.

Through the window, Ward spotted his mother and two sisters. He'd never seen a better welcoming committee. He would've liked Pa to have come, but knew the work it took to run a ranch. He grabbed his satchel and rushed from the train into female laughter and tears.

"We were so worried when we got your call." His mother cupped his face. "But the good Lord brought you home."

Ward planted a kiss on her forehead. "For now."

"You aren't staying?" Her brow wrinkled.

"Haven't decided. I figured I'd leave that decision up to the good Lord." He opened his arms, and his sisters, Lucy and Caroline, stepped into them. Caroline wore the traditional uniform of the Harvey House head waitress.

"There's your newest, sis." Ward motioned his head toward the girls milling on the platform. "They're a bit hungry for husbands."

She sighed. "Most of them are." She grinned up at him.

"I'm glad you're home. Come by the restaurant for supper. Since I'm here, I'd best go greet the girls." She hurried away.

Lucy grabbed his hand. "We brought the buckboard. Something's wrong with the automobile. Pa said it's more trouble than it's worth, and you should never have purchased it for us."

"I'll take care of it." Ward laughed. Pa had resented the motorcar from the moment Ward had bought it.

"No, you will not." His mother grabbed his arm. "You are home to get better, not struggle with a dirty machine. Of course, if healing means you'll be back getting shot, I hope it takes a good long while for you to recuperate."

Oh, it was good to be home. With his family clustered around him, Ward made his way to the wagon and climbed onto the seat. "I'll drive."

Ma sighed. "It's no use. You always were a poor invalid."

"When was I ever an invalid?" He was rarely sick, and this was his first, and hopefully last, bullet.

"I just want the chance to take care of you."

"And you have it." He watched as Caroline led her girls to the restaurant across the street. The dark-haired beauty glanced his way and turned back quickly when she caught him looking.

What was that girl's story? It might be interesting to find out. Something to look forward to while he waited for his side to stitch back together. With a flick of the reins, he set the horses for home.

His sister and mother chattered the whole way. Ward certainly had missed home. When they pulled in front of the house, Pa came running from the barn.

"Ward!" He held up a hand to help him down. "Easy, son."

"I'm fine, Pa. Just a little stiff." Actually, the jostling

ride home hadn't done his side much good at all. Fire burned from one side to the other.

"Don't lie. Hattie, get this boy some food and get him into bed." Pa grabbed Ward's bag.

Ma nodded. "Exactly what I planned on doing. Come on, Lucy."

"I'm fine." Ward fell into a rocker on the porch. "I'd like to sit here a spell, if that's all right."

"Lucy!" Pa bellowed. "Come sit with your brother. I've cows to feed." He placed a hand on Ward's head and then headed back to the barn.

Lucy seemed more than happy to oblige and sat at Ward's feet. "Tell me all about your adventures." The thirteen-year-old was still more child than she wanted to admit. "Did you meet any of the new Harvey Girls? I want to be one of them someday."

"Don't you have enough work here at home?" Ward winked. "I only ran into one of them, and she was a beauty."

"You didn't get her name?"

"No, I didn't. There wasn't time."

"Ma will be so disappointed." Lucy rested her chin on his knee. "They're so modern and glamorous."

"They work very hard. You know that. Look at Caroline." The last thing he wanted was for his starry-eyed younger sister to take up an occupation she had no realistic knowledge of.

"I work hard here. Caroline meets all kinds of people. I only know the people at school and church."

"All of Somerville."

"I want to meet *new* people from different places."

Ward rested his head back. Oh, the idealism of youth. He'd seen more atrocities in his twenty-seven years than he would ever tell his innocent sister. Or Ma. They didn't need to know the brutality of battle or how it felt to shoot a man, criminal or not. Thank the good Lord there was still beauty in the world.

He dozed off with the image of a brown-eyed girl in his mind.

Chapter 2

Having left Amos's money with the post office to be delivered after she left town, Katie didn't have that guilt hanging over her head. She hadn't needed the money after all. The Harvey Company paid all her expenses to Somerville. Even though she had returned his few coins, she didn't doubt that Amos would try to find her. After all, the coins were a meager few. It was the deed he wanted. Her safety had to stay in God's hands.

After less than a week as a Harvey Girl, she couldn't remember ever having worked so hard. With a smile, she set a plate of eggs in front of one customer and rushed to the next. There wasn't a part of her body that didn't ache. Least of all her feet. Sunday—her day off—had never looked so good. Katie planned on sleeping most of the day.

"Good morning, Katie." The head waitress smiled and patted Katie's shoulder on her way to the kitchen.

Some of the girls had spoken of stern, even mean, head waitresses, and Katie counted herself lucky. Sure, Miss

Alston expected hard work and excellent moral behavior, but she enforced it by being a living example. She didn't ask anything of her workers she didn't do herself.

Miss Alston returned. "Can you deliver this plate to table five? One of the girls took ill."

"Certainly." Katie took the plate of steak and eggs. Her steps faltered. The Ranger. She set the plate in front of him and turned to go. If she moved fast enough…

"Wait, please." He touched her elbow. "What is your name? We met in Houston, remember?"

"I remember." How could she forget? The sight of his star had almost frightened her to death. "I'm Katie." *Please, don't ask me a lot of questions.*

"Ah, you're the one." He grinned. "My sister, Miss Alston, speaks highly of you."

They'd been talking about her? That couldn't be good. Katie forced a smile. "I try hard. Please, excuse me." Her heart threatened to burst free. *Wait a minute. Did he just say the head waitress is his sister?* The man would be in all the time, then. What if he discovered Katie's secret? Found out she took the money? Sure, she'd returned it, but there was no telling what story Amos would make up.

Her hands shook as she continued serving breakfast. A slice of bacon slid from a plate onto the spotless table-cloth of her next customer, leaving a greasy stain. "I am so sorry." Katie grabbed the bacon. "I'll return with more." She raced to the kitchen.

The week's work would all have been for nothing if she didn't get ahold of herself. She sagged against the counter, ignoring the curious stares of the cooks. Could Amos have discovered her destination? Maybe she hadn't changed trains enough. It had to be Houston. She'd taken a terrible gamble returning the money, but she couldn't live another day with the theft hanging over her head. Lord, have mercy.

"Katie?" Miss Alston put an arm around her shoulder. "Are you all right?"

"Just a moment of weakness. It won't happen again." Katie straightened, grabbed a clean plate and stacked three slices of bacon on it. "I dropped a customer's bacon and need to replace it."

Miss Alston searched her face. "When the breakfast crowd leaves, step outside for a breath of fresh air. You look pale."

"Yes, ma'am." Katie hurried back to the waiting customer, avoiding eye contact with Mr. Alston. Surely, he would see guilt written across her forehead. She should have assumed an alias. Now it was too late.

"It's not possible. Not our Katie." Caroline handed Ward back the slip of paper on which he'd written a message.

"My captain gave me her name, not just an obscure description." Ward couldn't believe he had misread the shy girl when he'd found out her name. A thief? Even he found it hard to believe. "What does she do after supper each evening?"

"She reads in the parlor after taking a walk around town."

"Unsupervised?"

Caroline's shoulders slumped. "She's so quiet and solitary, I didn't see the harm in it. Most of the girls do pursue their own interests when they're off work."

"Be in the parlor tonight. I'll come visit you." He agreed that Katie didn't seem to fit the role of a criminal, but looks could be deceiving. He would need to hold judgment until he knew her better.

"If you insist, but I refuse to believe she's a crook." She glanced to where Katie folded napkins. "There must be some mistake."

"I hope so." He folded the paper and stuck it in his

pocket. "But a man named Amos Moore says she stole a land deed from him in Missouri, and quite a lot of money."

"There are better ways of hiding from someone than here at the Santa Fe, a busy railroad hotel and restaurant." Caroline crossed her arms. "That doesn't look suspicious to me."

"Maybe she thought an ordinary job out in the open would throw the law off her scent." He stood and tossed his napkin on top of his half-eaten steak. His appetite had fled at the woman's mention of her name, and she had been visibly shaken at the sight of him. That was a sure sign of guilt in his book.

His boots clunked on the polished floor as he exited the restaurant. He needed to phone his captain and let the man know the woman was indeed in Somerville and that Ward would investigate, unofficially of course. He was on medical leave, after all.

Having fixed the Model T Ford yesterday, he cranked it and slid behind the wheel. He missed riding a horse, but the car was smoother. Not a lot, but every little bit helped when it came to jostling his side.

He'd take the long way home in order to gather his thoughts. Ma would have a conniption if she knew he was working during his recuperation. Job or not, she wouldn't like it.

There had to be some way of finding out the truth. He'd always prided himself on his ability to read people. He couldn't have lost his touch, could he? Been swayed by a pretty face? Maybe finding a way to spend time in Katie's presence would give him some clues to her innocence…or guilt.

The visit with Caroline that evening would be a good start. Maybe he should bring Lucy. That little chatterbox could draw anyone into a conversation. The trick would be getting Katie to let down her guard and trust him. Thankfully, the captain hadn't given a deadline. Just that Ward should "unofficially" investigate until he found something that pointed to the woman as the culprit.

The stress of the day sent Katie outside. She hadn't intended to take her nightly stroll through the pastures surrounding Somerville, on account of her aching feet, but oh, the blessed summer breeze called her name. Lifting her face to enjoy the fresh air, the scent of honeysuckle reached her, along with the drone of bees.

After her walk, she planned to retire to the company parlor and read. Maybe a make-believe world could take her out of her terrifying one, if only for a while.

Her skirt stirred up dust along the lane, and she gave a halfhearted kick at a rock. She liked working for the Harvey Company, and loved Miss Alston and the other girls, but maybe she needed to think of asking for a transfer. After only a week. What would they think of her?

She covered her face with her hands. Papa would roll over in his grave if she gave up her work ethic. Most likely had already rolled over many times in the past few years, especially after Mama married Amos, and the man gambled away the small bit of money Papa had left to them. Other than the land and the small cabin, they had nothing to their name.

Then, Mama had died from consumption, Amos had discovered the hiding place of the deed without an owner's signature, and things had gone from bad to worse. Mama would never want Katie to sell the land that had been in their family for generations. She needed to keep possession of it. The only way she'd ever sell was if she gave up hope of ever returning.

The moon winked from behind the clouds, signaling that it was time to return to the hotel. Katie patted her hair back into place. An automobile motor rumbled in the distance, disturbing the silence. What if she kept walking? Left everything behind? She couldn't. Heart heavy, tears stinging her eyes, Katie shuffled to the parlor and chose her favorite chair by the fireplace.

The summer heat didn't warrant the use of a fire, but Katie hoped by choosing the same seat each night she would have the luxury once winter set in. Not that southern Texas was bound to get very cold, but surely it would have a chilly night or two. The crackle of a fire was one of the most soothing things in the world. She pulled the unfinished book from her pocket and settled back to escape.

"I finally get to see where the Harvey Girls spend their free time." A young girl with auburn curls bounced into the room, followed by Miss Alston.

"Respect people's privacy, Lucy." Miss Alston gave Katie a smile and perched on the edge of the settee.

"I'm Lucy Alston." The child held out her hand to Katie.

"I'm Katie." She returned the smile before going back to her reading. Heavier footsteps caused her to look up again.

"And we've already met." Hazel eyes gazed down at her. The Ranger.

"Ward, you said you didn't know any of the girls." Lucy planted her fists on her hips. "You're keeping information from me."

"I'm not. I only saw them from afar. Besides, some people do keep secrets, little sister." His gaze never left Katie's as he sat across from her. "It's a fact of life."

Katie squirmed. The peaceful evening had shattered. She stood, her fingers tired from gripping the book. "I'll leave y'all to your visit."

"No, don't leave." Lucy pouted. "I have so many questions."

"Shush." Miss Alston frowned. "Or I won't allow you in again. I apologize, Katie."

"That's a pretty name." Lucy grinned. "What are you reading?"

"Jane Eyre."

"Where are you from?"

"Missouri." Katie sat back down. Why all the questions? She prayed for a diversion so she could make her escape. It didn't help that the handsome Ranger wouldn't take his eyes off her. Katie had never been one of those girls who were flattered by a man's attention. She preferred the quiet life of home, church and books.

"Why did you want to be a Harvey Girl? I want to be one when I grow up."

"It's a respectable job." She shrugged. "I need to make a living."

Ward's eyebrows rose at her answer. Was it not respectable? Katie glanced at Miss Alston. Surely a Texas Ranger wouldn't allow his sister to work anyplace that was not respectable.

"Do you have family?" Lucy moved to a seat closer.

"No, my family is all gone."

"I have a lot of family. They treat me like a child."

"Maybe you shouldn't act like one." Ward laughed and ruffled her hair.

Katie flinched.

The move didn't escape the man's attention. His eyes narrowed.

And the covert glances between Ward and Miss Alston didn't escape Katie's attention either. It felt as if the two had the child interrogating her like a witness in a courtroom. Enough was enough.

Katie stood again. "It was a pleasure making your acquaintance, Miss Lucy. Mr. Alston. Miss Alston. I will retire to my room now." She nodded and left as if her heels were on fire.

Once outside the room, she planted a hand on the wall

and struggled to breathe. They suspected something. If she were to leave Somerville now, she would as good as announce her guilt. The only thing she was guilty of was taking a bit of money, and she'd made arrangements to have it sent back to Amos before she left town. She couldn't be arrested now, could she? The land, and the oil on it, was hers. Mama had said so. Mama would never have told Katie an untruth.

The problem was, since her pa hadn't known how to read or write, he had signed the deed with nothing but an *X*. Katie feared anyone could try to take away what he'd worked so hard to obtain—and that someone was Amos. Evidently he had another document saying Pa had sold him the land. But if Pa had sold him the land before he'd died, Amos surely wouldn't have married Katie's mother.

Oh, it was all so confusing, but Katie was sure of one thing: Amos wanted the creek that cut through Pa's acreage and the oil that lay under its fertile surface, and he would stop at nothing to get it. He'd already tried to lay hands on it by marrying Katie's mother. He'd also laid hands on Katie, and now he bore the scars to prove it. No, she'd do her best to keep out of the man's reach until she could prove the second paper was a forgery. But how could she do that?

Maybe she could confide in Mr. Alston? No. If he was prone to jumping to conclusions, or apt to take a bribe like some lawmen she knew, he might take Amos's word over hers.

Lord, help me. Please. One way or the other, she needed a resolution. She couldn't continue to live under such stress.

She glanced at the book in her hand. The love story within its pages failed to lift her spirits. Instead, her spirit was heavy. There would be no sleeping in late the next morning. Katie needed church more than she ever had before. Ma had always told her that God's presence held the answers to life's problems.

Katie longed to be soothed by God's Word. Regret over leaving behind Mama's Bible filled her, but the large book with a list of the births and deaths of generations of Gambles had been too large to bring along. Maybe the town's church could lend her a Bible.

Steps heavy, Katie made her way to her room. Sarah and Rachel's excited chatter reached her through the door. She had to compose herself before entering. She absolutely could not let them see her upset or the two would jump on her like birds on a bug.

Taking a deep breath, Katie squared her shoulders and opened the door. "Evening, ladies."

"Enjoy your read?" Rachel looked up from a stocking she was darning. "I am so glad to have our first day off. I plan to lounge all day."

"I'm going to visit the mercantile," Sarah said. "I need some toilet water."

"Neither of you attend church?" Katie set the book on her dresser.

"Not unless someone makes me," Rachel admitted. "I'm a good person. I see no need for someone to point out what a sinner I am."

"But church is so much more than that." Katie sat and unlaced her shoes.

Rachel shrugged, bit off the end of her thread, then rolled the stocking. "Time for me to get to sleep. No early morning alarm for me either."

"Or me." Sarah giggled, climbing under her covers. "I'll go to church next week, Katie. We aren't all heathens here. I just haven't had a chance yet to see what the town has to offer."

Katie reached behind her to unfasten her dress. Keeping her back to the girls so they wouldn't see the pocket pinned to her undergarments, she slipped her nightgown over her head, then finished undressing.

Secrecy was worth the teasing she got from the other two girls over her modesty. Climbing into bed, she prayed the questioning she received from the Alston family wouldn't keep her awake.

Maybe she should befriend them, as painful as it would be. Papa had always said a person should keep their enemies close.

Was Ward Alston a friend or an enemy?

Chapter 3

"If you'll tie my bow, I'll tie yours," Katie offered on Monday morning, as she watched Sarah struggle to get her apron tied correctly.

"Bless you." Sarah dropped the strings and turned her back. "No matter how hard I try, I can't get it big and fat like the head waitress likes."

The tying of aprons should have been the least of Katie's worries with the threat of losing everything looming over her head.

She patted Sarah's shoulder. "There you go, tied up like a Christmas package."

"Maybe so, but you're the one that's as pretty as a gift. Dark hair and eyes that would make any man swoon." Sarah giggled. "I couldn't help but notice the Ranger could hardly take his eyes off you during breakfast."

Katie struggled not to flinch. She couldn't let the other girl know how much her comment worried Katie. "Don't make something into something it isn't. Turns out his little sister wants to be a Harvey Girl someday and has chosen me to pester."

"Maybe so." Sarah tightened the bow. "But I know admiration when I see it."

"Stop talking nonsense. There's work to do." With a last glance in the mirror to make sure the bow in her hair was straight, Katie was satisfied and led the way to the dining room. Miss Alston had told her yesterday she'd work the lunch counter today. Hopefully, the Texas Ranger preferred to take his meals at a table.

"Good morning." She greeted her first customer and filled his mug with coffee. "What can I get for you?"

The man rattled his paper, keeping it in front of his face. "Just the coffee. I'm only passing through."

Katie frowned. He wouldn't be the last customer to be rude, but since the women did work on tips in addition to their salary, she hoped they'd at least look at her. "That's fine, sir. Let me know if I can serve you later." She moved to the next customer along the counter.

"Don't worry." Miss Alston lifted the lid on the coffeemaker. "They're not all friendly." She smiled. "Thank you for indulging my sister and her questions Saturday night. I'm afraid Lucy went home with stars in her eyes about the glamorous job of a Harvey Girl."

"I enjoyed talking to her." It was the older brother that sent prickles down Katie's spine. She glanced at the door, half expecting him to march in and arrest her.

"My brother just returned from the battle at San Benito and is recovering from his wounds. Between him and this restaurant, Lucy is convinced her life is as dull as mud. Keep up the good work." She patted Katie's shoulder and moved through the kitchen doors.

Katie hadn't realized how tense she'd gotten through the conversation. Now her neck ached from holding herself so rigid. How would she ever manage to live in such close contact with a Ranger and his family? She was doomed, and bound to be arrested the moment the man found out why she'd fled to Somerville.

How could she prove the land belonged to her? Why hadn't her parents learned to read and write? They'd been very concerned about Katie getting schooled. Said they wanted the finest things in life for their only child.

Well, their plans had failed. Now Katie was on the run from a ruthless man and doomed to a life of looking over her shoulder. Pa would have never sold the land to a man like Amos. Not if he'd known the true nature of the man he'd called friend. A nature that rose to the surface mere weeks after Ma had married him.

Lord forgive her, she didn't mean to be ungrateful for her parents' sacrifice. Really, she didn't.

She patted her pocket for the umpteenth time that morning, just to feel the reassuring crinkle of paper.

"Hello, darling. Did you miss me?"

Katie dropped the coffee carafe and stared into the scarred face of Amos Moore. One scar, still red from where she'd hit him with a porcelain pitcher, caused his left eye to droop. "How'd you find me?" She detested the waver to her words, the hoarseness of her voice.

"Wasn't hard. Folks back in Possum Springs know just about everyone. It's hard to forget a woman with looks like yours no matter where you stop along the railroad." He held up his mug. "Can't a man get a drink around here?"

She whirled for a fresh pot of coffee. Could she run? She eyed the door, and froze. Ward Alston's large frame blocked the light.

Ward stopped just inside the restaurant door and surveyed the room. Katie stared back, looking like a deer that had just caught scent of a predator. He grinned and moseyed her way, taking the last seat at the counter. "Good morning, Katie." He nodded at the man next to him.

The stranger glanced at the star on Ward's chest, slapped some coins onto the counter, and skedaddled. Ward raised his eyebrows and focused his attention on Katie. "Do you know him?"

She shook her head and ducked behind the counter.

What a strange girl. Ward leaned over the counter. "What are you doing down there?"

"I dropped a pitcher." She kept her head down. "I need to clean it up before someone is injured."

Ward sat back and scratched his head. He'd wager a dollar that Katie knew the stranger, and wasn't happy to see him. In fact, she'd looked downright terrified. He turned around and glanced out the window.

Sure enough, the man stared through the window but dashed away when Ward caught him staring. What kind of trouble had Katie Gamble brought to his town? First the telegram, now an unscrupulous character. Maybe he shouldn't let Lucy anywhere near the woman.

He stood and waited outside the kitchen door until his sister appeared. Grabbing Caroline by the arm, he pulled her into a small hall. "I want you to keep an eye on Katie."

Caroline tried to peek around the corner, and glared when Ward yanked her back. "Whatever for? Are you still believing that sweet girl is a crook?"

"She waited on a man who looked like he was up to something. My instincts about a man's character are rarely wrong when that man is no good. When I asked Katie if she knew him she said no. I don't believe her. She looked frightened."

"Please." Caroline backed up. "He probably said something that scared her. Some of the men do, but most are harmless. She'll get used to it." She crossed her arms. "What does the man look like? I'll have him refused service if it bothers you so much."

"He's heavyset, about six foot, a scar down the left side of his face." Ward gripped her arms. "I don't want you to be the one to deny him. Have the manager take care of it. I don't like the look of him." Nor the way he'd fled upon sight of Ward's badge.

She sighed. "You aren't acting like a lawman, Ward.... Oh, you like Katie and don't want to believe she's a crook either. Admit it."

"Yes, from what I've seen, she doesn't seem bad." But looks could be deceiving. Years of experience had taught him that. As for his sister's remark about his liking Katie, he would let those words slide. Sure, the woman was about the prettiest gal he'd ever seen, but it was never wise to have romantic notions about someone you were assigned to keep an eye on.

"I'll ask her a few questions about her customers. Find a seat close enough to hear, but not close enough to alarm her. You'll be lucky if I don't tell Mother you're working when you're supposed to be recovering from your wound." With a swish of her skirts, she left.

Tattletale. He had a job to do with or without a bullet hole in his side. He put a hand over the bandage. One that hurt. Maybe he should slow down.

He followed at what he hoped was a discreet distance and took a seat a few over from where he had sat originally. Katie was back at her station, smile in place, although still pale.

Caroline sidled up to her, a concerned look on her face. "Are you all right, Katie?"

"Yes." She drew the word out, her brows drawn together.

"That man seemed to be bothering you. Did you know him?"

"No, ma'am." She turned her head, suddenly busy with rolling silverware. "I've never seen him before."

Caroline glanced Ward's way and shrugged. He should have known she wouldn't press the issue. An interrogator his sister was not.

The bright spots of color on Katie's cheeks told of her lie. Ward held up his mug to be filled. With a sigh, she lifted the carafe and came to him.

"Thank you." He sipped the fragrant brew. Nothing like a good cup of coffee, and the restaurant made the best. Much better than the skunk water he drank in the field. And the waitresses were definitely better-looking than his fellow Rangers.

"You're welcome." She turned, then stopped and faced him. "Do you spend a lot of time in here?"

"Only when I'm home." He grinned.

"Are you home often?"

Wait. He was supposed to be asking *her* the questions. "Does my presence bother you?"

She shrugged. "Nobody who stays out of my business bothers me." She set down the carafe. "You appear to be settling in, so I'll leave the pot." With a nod, she retreated through the kitchen door.

Caroline laughed. "The girl's got some backbone, I'll say that for her. It's nice to see you put in your place."

"Oh, hush." Ward stared at the kitchen door. No longer a meek mouse, Katie might actually be fun to keep an eye on. But was the girl friend or foe? Only time would tell. "Is she allowed to leave her post like that or are you slacking on your job?" He grinned.

"Ha, ha, big brother." Caroline grabbed a rag and began wiping the counter. "She does as much work as two girls. I've no complaints. She'll be back…now."

Katie reentered with a full basket of clean linens.

"See, I never have to tell her what needs to be done

next." She leaned closer, her mouth near Ward's ear. "I don't think that's a common trait for a thief, do you?" She straightened and laughed. "Ma invited me for a late supper. See you later."

Sassy thing. He was surrounded by them. He watched as Katie efficiently folded napkins while having coffee ready the moment a man finished his cup. Pa always said still waters ran deep. Ward thought that might be true with Katie. He'd need to be careful with this job. The woman's dark hair and eyes would draw a man in as successfully as a spider trapping its prey.

Must he watch her so? Katie felt like a bug under a glass. It took every ounce of strength to continue working with that hazel gaze following her. If she didn't get away, her heart would burst right out of her uniform.

First Amos, then Ward. Her shoulders sagged. She straightened again as Ward narrowed his eyes. Maybe a strategically spilled coffee would make the man leave her alone. A smile twitched at her lips. She might imagine doing such a thing but never would. Not to a lawman.

She glanced at the window. The many times Amos had wandered past hadn't escaped her notice. Well, if the man was waiting for her to come out, he would have a long wait. She had no need to go anywhere until church, and that was days away. She'd miss her evening strolls, but… Her hand stilled in folding.

Had Amos taken that away, too? It wouldn't be safe to walk the lanes behind the hotel with him running loose. Why hadn't she brought Pa's pistol with her when she'd fled? No matter. She'd sneak out at the first opportunity and buy another. She had the bit of cash she'd received upon signing her contract.

She cut a glance at Ward, who still sat at the opposite

end of the bar. Would the man never leave? Shouldn't a wounded man be at home in bed?

But if he left, would Amos come back in? She was in a bind for sure. Either the lawman concerned about her actions, or the evil man after her land. Neither was pleasant. What a difficult choice for a girl to make.

One could land her in jail, and the other could have her killed.

Chapter 4

Katie knocked on the mercantile window, grateful the owner opened for the Harvey waitresses on Sunday afternoon. With her schedule, she had very few moments to shop.

Mrs. Freeman bustled to the door, wiping her hands on a ruffled yellow apron. She unlocked the door and held it open. "Katie, my dear. Come in. It's been a whole month since you've visited."

"My job keeps me busy. Thank you for opening for me. I believe a few of the other girls will be over in a bit." Katie returned the woman's infectious smile.

"As long as they knock hard, I'll hear them." Mrs. Freeman stepped behind the long polished wood counter. "What can I get for you today?"

Katie bit her bottom lip, and then took a deep breath. She hated for the kind woman to think ill of her, but she really needed something with which to defend herself. "I'd like a gun, please. Something small enough to fit in a woman's pocket."

Mrs. Freeman stared at her for a moment, and then nodded. "I suppose it is wise for a single woman to be able to defend herself. I have a Mauser pocket pistol that would be perfect." She reached under the counter and withdrew a wood box. "I can say this for the Germans—they do make a good gun. Can you shoot?"

"Very well." Katie took the weapon and tested its weight in her hand. "This will be perfect." Glancing around to make sure no one could see, Katie lifted her skirt and placed the gun in the hidden pocket in her petticoat. "It fits." She smiled into the startled look of the storekeeper.

After the initial shock, Mrs. Freeman laughed. "You'll be all right, Miss Katie. All right indeed."

The bump of the Mauser against her thigh reassured Katie as she stepped into the afternoon sunshine. She dared Amos to bother her now. She'd give him a scar on the right side of his face to match the left.

The town's church steeple rose white against the blue sky, reminding Katie that vengeance is the Lord's. She gave a nod toward the church and strolled down the wood sidewalks. She would do her best to avoid Amos, but she wouldn't lie down and let him hurt her. Not anymore. She wouldn't take vengeance, but she would protect herself.

"Katie!" Sarah practically skipped toward her with Rachel following at a more sedate pace. "Are you finished with your shopping already? If you don't mind waiting, the three of us could get something to eat at the diner."

"But we eat free at the restaurant." After purchasing the gun, Katie had little money left. Definitely not enough to splurge on something frivolous like a meal out.

Sarah looped her arm with Katie's. "But it's nice to eat somewhere else once in a while. Come on. I've a little extra. At least let me buy you a slice of pie."

Pie did sound nice. Katie's mouth watered. "Okay."

Rachel eyed her empty arms. "You didn't buy anything at the mercantile? Do you mind going back with us?"

She spotted Amos watching from the door of the livery and linked Rachel's arm in hers. "I don't mind." Their shoes made a pleasant staccato against the sidewalk as Katie marched the other two back to the store.

Mrs. Freeman gave her a questioning look, which Katie answered with a slow shake of her head. The woman nodded in understanding. "Welcome, ladies. How may I help you?"

"I need some buttons," Rachel said. "Preferably pearl. And I'd like to browse for an ornate hair comb."

"I want peppermint and ribbons," Sarah said, running her fingers through a bin of different colored hair ribbons.

Katie sidled to the side. She didn't want to be enticed into purchasing something she couldn't afford. She drifted toward the postal side of the store where a handful of wanted posters hung on a nail. If she found her face staring back at her she'd rip it down. She lifted the pages, one by one, praying she wouldn't have to break the law in order to maintain her independence. She wasn't guilty of anything and needed time to prove her innocence.

"This rose chiffon dress would look lovely with your complexion, Katie." Sarah held up a beautiful high-necked embroidered dress. "It's only two dollars and fifty cents."

"Two dollars and fifty cents I don't have at the moment. My dress is perfectly fine." She ran a hand down the navy suit she wore. Relieved at not finding her name or likeness on any of the pages, she turned back to her friends.

Friends. When was the last time she'd had any? Not for the six months Ma was married to Amos, that was for sure. The man had run the house with a heavy hand during the six months before Ma's death. A hand he often used against Ma and Katie for the smallest slight.

She moved to the counter, eyeing the bright colored

candies in glass jars. Maybe she could splurge. A handful of lemon drops sounded divine, and it had been so long. "I'll take some of those." She rubbed her hands together in anticipation.

Mrs. Freeman laughed. "Sweetheart, those happen to be on sale today. One pound for the price of a half."

The woman had lied for Katie's benefit and she loved her for it. "Thank you so much. A pound it is." She dug several coins out of her purse and dropped them into Mrs. Freeman's hand. "You're a true blessing."

Katie turned, clutching the bag containing her treasure, and froze when her gaze connected with Wade's as he watched her through the store window.

Now why would a young girl like Katie be interested in wanted posters? Wade watched as she chatted with two other women. She definitely didn't look like a crook, but would an innocent person flip through the posters? He shook his head in confusion. His boss wasn't wrong about the information he'd received. Something was not what it seemed with Katie Gamble.

He opened the door to the mercantile and stepped inside, tipping his hat to the four women. "Good afternoon, ladies. Mrs. Freeman, Ma said you told her I could pick up her order even though it's Sunday?"

Two of the Harvey Girls giggled and fluttered their eyelashes, but Katie stood there, pale-faced, her dark eyes wide as she watched him. His skin prickled. He felt like a bug in a jar with her unblinking gaze focused so intently on him. If he meant to find out any information from the wary girl, he'd need to find a way to get her to let down her defenses.

He gathered his mother's order of flour and sugar, then with another nod at the three staring women, marched back into the afternoon sunshine. One woman looked at him as if he wanted to hurt her, and the other two looked at him as if he were a side of beef. He didn't care for either look. He was in town to physically heal, do a job, then get back to work.

He set Ma's purchases in the back of his automobile and then headed to the church to pick up Lucy. She'd stayed after the service to help with a Sunday school lesson for the younger children, and she loved riding in the Ford.

He set the brake in front of the church and honked. Getting out, and then recranking the starter, pulled on his stitches. He prayed the pastor would forgive him his rudeness this time. After the second honk, Lucy tore down the stairs.

"You brought the automobile. Oh, my friends will be so jealous." She hopped onto the front seat and waved at two girls standing on the top step. "See you at school!"

"Don't gloat," he told her. "If not for my income, our family wouldn't be able to afford this either."

"I know, but it's just that Peggy got a new dress last week, and she's worn it three times. That's boasting." Lucy picked at a thread on her wool skirt.

"Maybe she only has a couple of dresses."

She shrugged. "Maybe, but she could definitely stop twirling, don't you think?"

Wade laughed. "She could definitely stop doing that." He steered the vehicle toward home, pleased to be behind the wheel. While he loved his horse, there was something about the automobile that tugged at him. The modern conveyance was a step into the new century.

"Look. There's Katie," Lucy hollered as she waved. "She's with two other girls. Are they Harvey waitresses, too? Oh, I can't wait until I'm eighteen."

Katie stumbled, whipping her head in their direction. She gave a small smile and returned the wave. Ward frowned. The woman could act a little more pleased to return the greeting of a young girl.

"Don't be in too big of a hurry to grow up," Ward said. "Enjoy being a child as long as possible."

"I'm not a child." Lucy crossed her arms and slouched against the seat.

At home, he parked the car next to the barn and grabbed his mother's purchases before following his rambunctious sister into the house. The tantalizing aroma of roast beef and gravy greeted him at the door. As soon as he'd set the flour and sugar on the kitchen counter, Ma waylaid him.

"Oh, good, you're home." Ma thrust a stack of plates into his hands. "Caroline is working so there're only four of us. I don't understand why the restaurant doesn't close on Sunday."

"The railroad doesn't, and people still need to eat." Ward set a plate at each setting. "She and the manager take turns watching over the girls. Let's be thankful she doesn't work every Sunday."

"You're right." Ma patted his cheek. "But I like all my babies around me. Go fetch your pa, okay? He's in the barn."

He grinned, knowing he was quite a few years past being a baby, and headed back outside. Pa was in the first stall, digging a pebble out of a horse's shoe. "This is why you should have a Ford." Ward squatted next to him.

"Then you get a flat." Pa patted the horse and let it place its foot on the ground. "I prefer something that gives back a little love."

Ward couldn't disagree. He loved the horse he rode while working, and missed the big black Mustang. "Ma sent me to tell you it's time to eat."

Pa nodded. "I'm so hungry my stomach thinks my throat's been cut." He led the way to the small mudroom off the kitchen and the two men washed their hands and faces before entering the kitchen. Most of the time, the family ate in the big farm kitchen, but on Sundays and holidays, Ma wanted them around the table in the dining room.

"They looked so stylish," Lucy was saying. "I bet they make all kinds of money being a Harvey waitress. Katie's as pretty as a dream, and she waved at me."

Ward shook his head and sighed. Lucy would be devastated if Katie Gamble turned out to be a crook. "They get paid less than your sister," he said, ruffling her hair. "I don't think they're as loaded as you imagine. If you don't romanticize the occupation, you won't be disappointed if you actually get hired." He'd be willing to bet something else would come along to attract his little sister. Like a young man. Maybe he preferred she be a waitress after all.

Ma set the roast on the table and handed Pa the knife so he could carve the meat. "Don't discourage your sister, Ward. I wouldn't mind meeting these lovely ladies myself. I should encourage Caroline to bring one of them home once in a while. What do you think? Everyone can use a home-cooked meal on occasion."

His ma had just made his job a whole lot more difficult.

Chapter 5

Katie ducked around the corner, leaned against the splintery wood wall of the mercantile and closed her eyes. Had he seen her? The deep shadows between the saloon and the store should make it easy for her to blend in with her dark-colored clothing. Just moments before she would have passed the open saloon doors, Amos stepped out.

Katie opened her eyes, her gaze falling on the church steeple rising above the buildings. Sanctuary waited within its whitewashed walls, but she'd never be able to make it that far before he caught her.

Why couldn't every day be Sunday? She felt safe within the walls of a church. She patted the gun in her pocket. Now with her gun she had a new way to feel safe.

"Give me the papers." Amos darted around the corner and grabbed her arm. "I know you have them. A nervous little thing like you wouldn't leave them anywhere but on your person." He used his free hand to pat her down.

Katie shrieked and landed the toe of her pointed boot

on his shin. "I have nothing that belongs to you. I made arrangements to have your money returned to you, and the deed is mine. Get your hands off me." She hefted her skirts and grabbed the Mauser. She aimed the weapon between his eyes. "Leave me alone or I'll put a bullet between your eyes."

"You don't have the guts. Besides, I never got the money. You're lying." He put his hands above his head and grinned as if she were playing a game. The hard glint of his eyes froze her blood.

"That is no concern of mine. I'm telling the truth. Take it up with the postal worker I paid to return it to you." She pressed the barrel hard enough against his head. "Do you really want to try me? I've nothing to lose. You've taken everything from me."

Please, go away. Amos was right. She wasn't sure she could actually pull the trigger on a person. Her hand trembled.

He laughed. "Watch your back, little girl. There will come a time when I catch you unaware."

"I'll be waiting."

He slapped the gun away from his head. "The papers I possess look more authentic than the pitiful one in your possession. Who do you think the law will believe? Me, an upstanding citizen, or a girl accused of theft?"

Katie lifted her chin, keeping a firm grip on the Mauser. "Let's take it to the law then."

He laughed, the sound as lacking in humor as a wolf's howl. "I've a few secrets I'm not ready to divulge just yet. We'll settle this between the two of us." He patted her cheek roughly, then turned and left.

Katie's knees refused to hold her, and she sagged against a nearby crate. She needed to leave town. Find a place where he could never find her. Someday, sometime, his nefarious ways would catch up with him and she'd be free. Until then…she needed to stay as far away from him as possible. There could not be a repeat of today. He could have easily bested her.

Maybe he didn't actually believe she kept the papers on her person and waited for her to divulge their hiding place. The longer she kept her distance from him, the more time she had to prove her innocence. She just needed to figure out how.

She slid the gun back into her pocket and stepped from the alley to glance up and down the main street of Somerville. She didn't want to leave the place. She already held a fondness for the cotton town and its simple people. Maybe she could continue her regular evening stroll in the meadow behind the hotel instead of here, but she'd thought it safe to walk among the townspeople.

The setting sun cast a shade of crimson on the church steeple, and drew Katie like a butterfly to a fragrant flower. She stopped in front of the building and craned her neck. Red, like the blood of her Lord, promising mercy. She moved up the steps and tried the door handle. Locked. Fitting. She might have thought herself in the right, but she was little more than a thief. She'd returned most of Amos's money, but she'd stolen it first, all the same. Would he leave her alone if she gave him the proceeds of her next pay and the money she'd put aside for the past month? She doubted it. It would never be enough money for him. He was looking for more than a young girl's salary. The man was playing a game—one he seemed to enjoy.

She tried to justify the act of taking his money by reminding herself that he'd stolen from her first, and he'd taken something more valuable than a few dollars. Still, stealing was going against God's commandments. Was Amos lying about receiving the money she sent back? If not, then it was her fault he didn't have it. If she hadn't taken the coins in the first place, they would never have been lost. Remorse struck her. How fitting that the church doors were locked. She didn't feel she deserved to find her solace there.

Blinking back tears, she turned to leave.

"Katie? Are you all right?" Ward stretched a hand toward her.

Why must he always find her at her weakest? Katie's hand clutched the lace at her throat and her heart pounded in her ears. Had he finally come to arrest her?

The girl paled and jumped back, those magnificent eyes wide and dark, focused on him in terror. His heart lurched. It pained him to have her look at him in such fear.

"I'm sorry if I startled you. Did you want into the church? Pastor Logan lives in that house over there." He pointed to a small white clapboard house next to the church. "He'll open for you if you ask him."

She shook her head, color returning to her face. "I'm fine. The moment has passed." She sidestepped around him and headed back down the street.

Ward caught up with her. "Are you going to the hotel? I'll walk with you. I intended to stop in for pie before heading home anyway." Pie had been the last thing on his mind after leaving the mercantile, but when he'd spotted Katie staring at the church steeple, she'd looked so lost and forlorn he couldn't help but see if she needed assistance.

After his trip to the store to purchase seeds for Pa, and discovering from the loose-lipped Mrs. Freeman that Katie had purchased a gun a few days ago, he'd intended to seek her out.

"Doesn't your mother bake?" Katie stopped and planted her fists on her hips. "Why purchase what you can get at home?"

Katie had a sharp mind. "Sometimes it's nice to get out of the house."

She mumbled something that sounded suspiciously like, "You're always out of the house."

He chuckled. Maybe he needed to be a bit more subtle about watching her comings and goings. If she suspected too strongly that he was investigating her, she might bolt. "I'm a wanderer. Being in Somerville recuperating is tough."

Their footsteps beat out a pattern on the sidewalk as Katie matched his steps. Once in a while her arm would brush his or the breeze would carry a whiff of her cologne, something flowery and clean, to his nostrils. If they'd met under different circumstances, Ward wouldn't have minded courting her. Someday. when he no longer worked as a Ranger.

He allowed Katie to go ahead of him up the stairs to the hotel, then he rushed ahead to open the door for her. She nodded. "Thank you. Enjoy your pie. I'll be retiring to my room."

After watching her march upstairs, Ward grinned and headed for the dining room. The restaurant would be closing soon, but maybe he could finagle that slice of pie from his sister.

"Ward." Caroline glanced up from her conversation with one of the other girls. "You're out kind of late."

"Got any pie leftover?" He slid onto a stool at the counter.

"Apple or pumpkin?"

"Apple, and a cup of coffee."

Caroline waved the waitress away and poured coffee into a mug. "What brings you into town this late?"

"Needed seeds for Pa and a part for the Ford." He blew into the fragrant brew in front of him. "Ran into Katie outside the church and walked her home."

His sister nodded. "She walks every night after her shift. Once I became aware of her habit, I let her start work before breakfast and end right after dinner. It gives her time for her walks and she seems to cherish her solitude."

"She doesn't get along with the other gals?"

"She gets along with them just fine, even seems pretty close to two of them." Caroline slid a plate with a slice of pie on top toward him. "Leave her alone, Ward. She's not a crook."

"That remains to be seen. Katie Gamble hides a secret behind that pretty face, and I aim to find out what it is." Not to mention her recent purchase of a gun. Ward forked off a piece of the warm flaky pie and took a bite. Not as good as Ma's, but still delicious.

Caroline waved a towel in his face. "If you mess up one of my best workers, I'll bash you with a skillet."

He held up his hands in surrender and laughed. "I'll be discreet."

"Sure you will." She scowled and stormed toward the kitchen, tossing a warning over her shoulder. "Watch it, big brother, or I'll tell Ma you're working."

His sisters always threatened to tell Ma. Ward shook his head. He had Ma wrapped around his little finger. As the only son, all he had to do was grin. Now, if he was to do something foolish and hurt a girl's feelings, that might warrant a wallop, but little else would.

What was it about Katie that made people want to protect her? Those big dark eyes? The petite frame? He had a feeling that the little woman had more strength and fortitude than a lot of folks gave her credit for. He'd seen inklings of it with his own eyes.

He really hoped she wasn't a crook and that somehow someone had gotten their facts wrong. He fished the telegram his boss had sent him from his pocket.

Check out a Katie Gamble. Harvey Waitress. Stop.
Five foot two inches. Stop. Dark hair and eyes. Stop.
Wanted for questioning regarding thievery claim.
Stop.

The information in his hand was matter-of-fact. There
was only one Harvey waitress with the name Katie Gamble
in this town who fit that description. Ward doubted there
was another at one of the other hotels down the line. No
matter what his sister said, he had no choice but to get to
the bottom of the accusation against the girl.

He didn't want her to be found guilty any more than
anyone else. Lovely and spirited, Katie was the type of
gal he would want to know better—under different circumstances. But right now, he had a job to do and one he
intended to do well. He slid off the stool. He wouldn't let
a pretty face get in the way.

Chapter 6

Amos sat on his usual stool. Every meal, he sat there and watched every move Katie made until she wanted to make real her threat to shoot him. Add in Ward spending a minimum of an hour at the hotel every morning nursing a mug of coffee, and Katie wanted to scream. Did nobody work in the town of Somerville?

"Why don't you go away and leave me alone?" she whispered insistently as she poured Amos's third cup of coffee. "See that man over there?" She motioned her head toward Ward. "He's a Texas Ranger, and if you don't stop haunting me, I'll—"

"A Ranger, huh?" Amos narrowed his eyes. "Perhaps I should have a talk with the man. Enlighten him as to what kind of woman he has in his town." He ran a finger over the healing wound on his face. "He might be interested in knowing how dangerous you really are."

"I've done nothing wrong." Her hand shook, and some of the coffee sloshed over the rim of Amos's mug, landing on his hand.

He leaped to his feet with a curse. "You did that on purpose!"

Tears stung her eyes. He'd say something to Ward for sure. "I didn't. It was an accident."

Ward didn't move. Instead, he watched them with shrewd eyes.

Caroline moved to Katie's side and dabbed Amos's hand. "The breakfast is on us, sir. Please forgive Katie. She's one of our best girls and not prone to clumsiness."

He brushed her hand away. "Then you might want to reevaluate your girls. She's a menace and a crook."

The blood drained from Katie's face all the way to her toes. It was out there now. The hateful accusation. Caroline would fire her for sure now. The Harvey Company would not employ anyone accused of thievery.

"You, sir, are out of line." Caroline pointed at the door. "Please leave or I will have to get the manager."

"You haven't heard the last of me." Amos whirled and stormed from the restaurant.

Katie sagged against the counter, her gaze meeting the sharp-eyed one of Ward. Her only hope was that he wouldn't arrest her in front of the breakfast crowd. She froze for a moment, and then bolted for the kitchen. Not stopping to answer questions from the chef or other girls, she continued outside and across the empty field behind the hotel.

Hitching her skirt to her knees, she ran until she found cover in a small stand of trees. Tears now running freely, she leaned against a tree trunk to catch her breath and wipe her face on her apron.

What should she do? She desperately needed the income from her job. If she put in for a transfer, how long would it be until she could leave? Wouldn't that make her appear more guilty? She rubbed her hands over the hidden pocket holding her gun and papers. Leaning her head against the hard trunk, she glanced through the branches toward heaven.

She had Amos's money. Since he said he doesn't have it, she would give him the small remaining amount when she saw him next. She needed to carry it with her so she could do just that. What more did the man want? Did he actually expect her to hand over to him what was left of her parents? She couldn't. Not ever. If only she could have found evidence to dispute his claim that her mother had signed over the land's oil rights to Amos. Even if she found out Amos was right, which would pain her to the core of her being, it would be better than this cat-and-mouse game they played.

What if the deed with Pa's *X* wasn't enough to give ownership to Katie? Pa had always said the land would go to her upon his death. Had he given it to Ma instead, assuming Ma would leave it to Katie upon her death? That would have worked just fine if Ma hadn't married Amos. She clasped her hands around her head, trying to still the drumming in her skull.

"Katie? Miss Gamble?" Ward's boots crunched through the underbrush as he made his way to her side.

Katie sniffed and raised her head. So, here he was. Would he take her by the arm and drag her off to jail? How silly of her to think that way. Maybe he wasn't here to arrest her but truly wanted to know if she was all right. Although his occupation frightened her, the man had been nothing but kind. Ward was the type of man Ma would have liked Katie to marry.

Her face burned. My, how her mind went off in strange directions sometimes. Her life was too unsettled to think about a relationship with a man. No matter how handsome and kind.

"My sister sent me to see if you are all right. If that man is bothering you, I can have the sheriff tell him to stay away."

"The sheriff?" *Why doesn't Ward step in if he thinks so?*

As if he'd read her mind, he continued. "I don't work out of Somerville and I'd hate to step on the sheriff's toes, but that man seems to frighten you. I'll ask you again if you know him? I am more than willing to step in. All you have to do is ask." Concern filled his gorgeous eyes.

There he went being all nice and friendly. His manner wasn't helping her keep her emotions in check. She took a deep breath. "He's my stepfather, Amos Moore. My parents are both now dead."

"I take it the two of you don't get along?" He crooked his arm. "Let me walk you back to the hotel while you regain your composure."

She placed her hand on his arm, feeling the hardness of his muscles. Maybe she could have a friend in the handsome Ranger. A protector against Amos.

"I'll be fine." What could she say to this lawman that wouldn't dig a deeper hole? She didn't want to lie. Falsehoods were too difficult to keep track of, not to mention that lying was a sin. She spent a lot of time repenting lately, it seemed. "We're battling over my inheritance. Nothing I can't handle, but each time I see him, it unburies the pain." She hoped Ward would accept her falsehood for wanting to avoid Amos. Friendly or not, Ward was a Ranger, and Katie wasn't ready to trust her future to his hands.

"What about an attorney?"

"I can't afford one. I'm trying to save all my pay, but it will take a long time. Right now, my job here, and the long hours it entails, are all I can handle." She glanced at the sun. "I've got to get back to work. Thank you for coming after me."

"Wait." He stopped her. "Caroline said you take walks each evening after work. Do you mind if I join you? At least until that man learns to stay away?"

She stared into his strong face and admired the hazel

eyes, shaded by his hat, the firm jaw and just a hint of a beard. He looked like everything she could want in order to feel safe, except for the badge she knew he carried in his pocket. What if his show of friendship was nothing more than a ploy to get her to give up information? But then, two could play at that game. She nodded and strolled away, tossing over her shoulder that she would meet him in the lobby at 6:00 p.m.

Ward grinned. The two of them had entered into a game, and he found himself excited to play. He'd seen the spark of awareness in her dark eyes. She intended to keep him close to find out what he knew just as he intended to keep her by his side in hopes of discovering her innocent or guilty of the accusations against her. He rubbed his hands together. Six o'clock wouldn't come soon enough.

Instead of heading home for the few hours until he met with Katie, he headed for the sheriff's office. It wouldn't hurt to put a bug in the sheriff's ear about Amos stalking Katie. If the man harassed her too much, she might pack up and leave and someone other than Ward would be made responsible for keeping an eye on her.

He made short work of the distance between the hotel and sheriff's office, and swung open the door to see Sheriff Lander, a rotund, red-faced man, sitting with his feet propped on his desk. He'd left his boots on the floor, and both pairs of socks sported holes. From the prominent blood veins in the man's bulbous nose, Ward suspected the man might spend more time in the saloon than behind his desk.

"Yep." Lander switched the toothpick in his mouth from one side to the other with his tongue. "What can I do you for?"

"There's a man bothering one of the gals at the Harvey

restaurant. He eats all his meals there and frequents the same place at the counter."

"Doesn't sound like that's against the law to me." The sheriff let the chair bang back onto all four legs. "Is he hurting her? You're a lawman. Why don't you put a stop to it?"

"I'm on a leave of absence and I don't want to butt into your territory without your permission."

"What's this man's name?"

"Amos Moore."

"Never heard of him. Is he wanted?"

Ward shrugged. "Name doesn't ring a bell."

"Then tell the fool to leave the girl alone and go on your way. I'm busy." The sheriff picked up a stack of papers.

A serious waste of time and flesh, that man. Maybe Ward should consider complaining to someone higher up. He barged back onto the sidewalk. Now, not only did he need to find out whether Katie was a crook, he needed to protect her from a man who may, or may not, intend her harm. So much for taking time off work. Ma was going to kill him.

He made his way to the telegraph office and sent a message to his supervisor that things were still unclear as to whether Katie was breaking any laws. He mentioned that another factor had entered the case and he might need more time. Work was work, whether he was riding the range or strolling along the sidewalks of Somerville. It all put a paycheck in his pocket and helped him put away the bad guys. With still an hour to go until he met Katie, Ward needed something to do other than purchase another cup of coffee.

Amos Moore ducked into a saloon down the street. Ward grinned. He didn't drink, but he could nurse a glass of sarsaparilla in order to keep an eye on the man. After glancing both ways before crossing the street, he jogged to the saloon.

All heads turned and conversation ceased as he pushed through the swinging doors. Tugging his hat low over his eyes, Ward bellied up to the bar and ordered his drink, then turned, leaning his elbows on the counter, and faced the room. The patrons turned back to their card games, no longer interested in another drinker.

Ward reached behind him and then lifted his glass to his lips, pretending to drink. The object of his scrutiny sat at a scarred wood table with three other men, all well within their cups and laughing raucously. To a casual observer, Amos would seem like an ordinary fellow who enjoyed his liquor, but the fact he dogged Katie's footsteps showed the man had a sinister motive. Instinct told Ward there was more to the man's charges than Katie stealing a few dollars. Both Katie and Amos would warrant regular surveillance. One of them more pleasant than the other.

After observing Amos for a while, he realized it was almost time to meet Katie. Leaving his empty glass, Ward pushed away from the bar and left the saloon by the back door, which took him by the table Amos sat at. The man laughed and tossed down some bills, saying he'd be coming into a lot of money soon and certain folks should pay attention.

Interesting. Using his index finger, Ward pushed his hat back from his eyes. This assignment was becoming more interesting every day.

He put a hand to the wound on his side. He'd overdone it that day, and the scar pulled.

Katie came out of the restaurant and stood on the top step, one hand shading her eyes. Ward smiled at the pretty picture she made in a light blue dress that swirled around her ankles. With her mass of dark hair piled on her head, she was a vision, for sure. He looked forward to spending time with her, investigation or not. He'd need to rely on the Lord to keep his heart out of the case and his mind centered.

"Good evening." He jogged toward her. "You look nice."

"It feels good to take off the uniform once in a while." A smile teased at the corners of her mouth, but didn't quite reach her eyes.

So, the lovely dress was for his benefit. She thought to throw him off the trail by looking too innocent to be guilty. He crooked his arm, more excited to dig deep into an investigation than ever before.

May the good man, or woman, win.

Chapter 7

Katie's heart thumped so hard, she thought for sure it would burst free and land in the dust at her feet. Spending time with Ward might not be one of the wisest decisions she'd ever made. Especially with the twinkle in his eyes when he glanced at her or the way his muscle bunched under her hand when she slipped her arm through his.

"Would you enjoy an ice cream?" Ward put his large hand over hers.

Her skin tingled. "Yes. I can't remember the last time I enjoyed such a treat."

"I thought we could head to the diner. You're probably tired of the hotel." Ward helped her navigate the busy street, leading her through the horses, buggies and the occasional automobile as if he had a sixth sense. "Then, we'll stroll the sidewalks and I'll introduce you to the town."

"Sounds wonderful." Why wasn't she better at the art of flirtation? Unless he asked her a question that required a direct answer, her tongue remained glued to the roof of her mouth. The good thing about being unable to speak was the fact that she wouldn't be able to say anything incriminating.

Gas streetlights, three to be exact, illuminated small areas of the sidewalk as the sun descended. With four hours until the appointed curfew for the Harvey Girls, Katie had plenty of time to perspire under Ward's gaze.

He opened the door to the diner and stepped back to allow her to enter first. The small room was crowded with families and couples. No empty tables offered a place to sit.

"It looks like we'll be walking while enjoying our treat," Ward said, stepping up to the counter.

Katie nodded and asked for a scoop of vanilla. While waiting, she gazed around the room, noticing several familiar faces from diners at the restaurant. Outside the large window, Sarah fairly skipped past, her arm linked with a man Katie didn't recognize. She smiled. Only one of the girls had broken her contract to run off into married bliss, but Katie suspected lively little Sarah might be announcing her engagement soon. After all, she'd been outspoken about her intentions to catch a husband.

"Here you go." Ward handed her a waffle rolled into a cone with a scoop of vanilla ice cream inside.

Ward opened the door and followed her outside. "There's a small park around the corner. Would you feel safe sitting there?"

She glanced up at him. "Of course. You're a Ranger. Anyone would feel safe with you." Of course, she'd feel secure with Ward if he weren't a Ranger. The man's sheer size and steely gaze ought to be enough to deter most folks from causing trouble. She frowned at having missed the perfect opportunity to flirt and play the helpless female.

"If I were that wonderful, I wouldn't be back here nursing a bullet wound." One side of his mouth quirked.

She shrugged and licked her ice cream. The cool creaminess of the treat melted on her tongue.

They passed the saloon, and two men fell out the door and rolled in the dirt while throwing punches at each other's faces. "Shouldn't you do something?"

Ward shook his head. "If they want to knock each other senseless, let them. If anyone is concerned they can get the sheriff. As long as there are no guns or knives involved, I won't break them up." He motioned toward another man storming toward them. "See? The sheriff can handle this."

Katie stepped into the shadows behind Ward. She hadn't met the sheriff yet, and didn't intend to for as long as she could prevent doing so.

The two men rolled onto the sidewalk, and Katie jumped out of their way. She knocked into Ward's back, the gun in her skirts banging against her leg. Unmindful of the ice cream in her hand, she held on to her skirts and hoped the gun hadn't hit Ward.

Her sudden movement smashed what was left of her ice cream against her clothes. She sighed and tossed the cone between two buildings, and then pulled a handkerchief from her purse to dab at the smeared dessert.

"Are you all right?" Ward took her by the elbow and guided her farther down the sidewalk.

"Yes, but stop and let me finish cleaning up." She pulled free. His determined steps and cold tone signified an unhappy man. While she swiped at her skirt, she cast him furtive glances, waiting for him to explode, as so many of the men she'd known usually did.

"My apologies." He stared down at her until she finished. Once she had wadded the handkerchief back into a ball and shoved it in her purse, he continued his march down the sidewalk, his hand firmly around her elbow.

"Are you angry with me?" Maybe Katie could ask Sarah to give her some tips on girlish behavior with a gentleman.

His steps faltered, and he sighed. "Again, my apology. No, I am not angry with you, and I'm sorry if I led you to believe I was. Please." He waved toward a bench under a willow tree. "Have a seat."

Katie sat ramrod-straight and bit her bottom lip. The bench under the tree, the faraway glow of a glass street-light, all led to a romantic atmosphere. How far would this handsome Texas Ranger go to elicit information from her? Would he try to kiss her? Hold her hand?

She twisted her fingers in the fabric of her skirt. No one had ever kissed, much less courted, Katie. No one wanted the girl from the mountain hollow. Not until Fred Harvey's company had hired her. Would a man ever want Katie for herself and not something she could do for him?

Most young men who had come around wanted her for her pa's land. Her family hadn't had money, but the land was prime and a magnet to local men wanting to improve their land holdings. Ward pretended to enjoy her company because he believed she'd committed a crime. Tears stung her eyes when he sat next to her, long legs stretched out in front of them.

Everything in her wanted to leap to her feet and run away.

Ward needed to shake off the sense of despair he'd felt when Katie had bumped into him. He'd noticed the unmistakable jab of something hard from under her dress. Considering his discovery of her gun purchase, he suspected that was what it was. If she was innocent, then why the need to carry a hidden weapon? He crossed his arms. Was it only a matter of time before he found himself on the receiving end of one of her bullets? Had she only agreed to accompany him in case the opportunity presented itself? Plenty of unscrupulous lovely ladies had no qualms about shooting someone if it meant maintaining their freedom. Still, he had a hard time lumping Katie in with that type.

Caroline would tell him he was the biggest fool who walked the earth. Maybe he was, but it was times like that that had him thinking the worst of Katie Gamble.

He made out her face through the darkness. Under the moonlight, her skin took on the hue of a fantasy world. His fingers itched to see if her skin was as velvety soft as it appeared. How could anyone with such beauty be a thief?

A woman screamed from across the park. Katie clutched his arm.

"Stay here." He removed her hand and stood.

"No." Her voice shook. "You can't leave me alone."

"Then stay behind me."

"Okay," she whispered, digging her nails into his upper arm. The girl was like a frightened cat. "Don't leave me. I can keep up." She relinquished her hold.

The scream came again, and Ward sprinted across the lawn toward the sound. True to her word, Katie was swift on her feet, despite her skirts. A cutoff scream spurred him faster toward his destination.

He burst through tall brush to see a woman on the ground and a man straddling her. His hand covered the woman's mouth. She turned frightened, tear-filled eyes in Ward's direction.

"Sarah?" Katie shoved past Ward and launched herself at the stranger. "Get off her!"

Ward grabbed Katie around the waist and swung her behind him. Who was this woman? "I suggest you do as this gal says, mister, or I'll unleash her on you." Ward pulled his pistol. "She isn't as concerned about your welfare as I might be."

The man raised his hands above his head and got to his feet. Katie immediately rushed to Sarah's side.

Ward waved his gun. "Let's go, mister. You've got an appointment with the sheriff. Katie, you and your friend follow close behind, please."

"We will. As soon as Sarah is back to rights." Ward turned his back to give the women privacy. He gritted his teeth, imagining one of his sisters or Katie as the victim, and wanted to clobber the man in front of him. The man's breath washed over Ward's face with the stench of whiskey.

"We're ready," Katie said, glaring at the stranger as she shoved past.

"March, mister." Ward motioned for him to follow.

"I wasn't gonna hurt her." The man frowned. "We had a nice dinner, a drink or two, and I wanted a little more fun. She put out the right signals. What's a man supposed to think?"

"Her 'no' would have been a good indication she was no longer interested," Ward said.

"Or the first scream," Katie tossed over her shoulder. "You want me to hit him for you, Sarah?"

Ward bit his lip to keep a smile from breaking free. Katie Gamble might look like a lady, but he caught glimpses of a steel backbone the more time he spent with her. He wasn't sure which side of her he preferred, since both were equally endearing.

"Yes." Sarah's word shuddered. "In the nose."

Katie whirled and doubled her fist.

"No." Ward shook his head. "You're lucky I'm here, mister. I have a feeling these two would win a fight."

"He deserves it," Katie said. "A punch and more."

"Granted, but we'll let the sheriff handle him."

She huffed and turned back to Sarah, leaving Ward's spirits light despite the somber circumstances. Other than frightened, Sarah looked all right. They'd arrived in time to prevent anything worse than drunken kisses. Had the man been in the middle of... Well, Ward refused to allow his mind to go there. Let it be said that he wouldn't have been responsible for his actions had the man gotten further with the woman.

After several moments of pounding on the sheriff's door, the man finally answered it and took custody of Ward's prisoner. "He'll be out tomorrow."

Ward nodded. "For his own sake, I suggest he be very apologetic to the lady the next time he sees her." He returned his weapon to its holster and offered an arm to each lady. "It would be my honor to escort you both back to the dormitory."

Sarah sniffed, and nodded. "Thank you. I'll be fine. My nerves are a little rattled, is all."

"I'll make sure you stay in bed tomorrow," Katie said. "I'll take your place in the dining room. I'm sure Miss Alston won't mind."

"Caroline is headed to New Mexico for a week or two." Ward led them in a wide circle around the saloon. "I'm not sure who is filling in for her. Didn't she tell you?"

"Of course. I'd forgotten. She told us at supper." She put a hand to her head. "The evening is such a jumble now. Sarah and I will switch places," Katie said. "The lunch counter requires much less running back and forth."

"Thank you, Katie." Sarah stopped on the top step of the hotel. "And thank you, sir. You are a rare form of gentleman." With a swish of her skirts, she moved through the doors.

"Thank you, Ward. If we hadn't heard her scream—" Katie ducked her head.

"But we did." He took her hand, which was every bit as soft as he'd thought. "I may be stepping over my boundaries here, but I feel I must tell you..." He stared into her dark eyes, losing all train of thought.

"Yes." The one whispered word kissed his face.

"Please don't threaten to beat up a man again. You most likely wouldn't win." Although if he were a betting man, and he was not, he'd bet on the feisty waitress winning every time.

Chapter 8

Katie stopped and read the Harvey Company motto before heading downstairs. "Maintaining quality regardless of cost." How true. Something she, too, strived for in her job, but having never waited tables, her legs trembled. Please, Lord, don't let her spill anything on a customer.

Smoothing her apron, she followed several other girls to the restaurant and merged with the group as they received their morning instructions. A tall woman, on the verge of being described as bony, held herself erect in front of the group. "I am Head Waitress Dunlap. I am filling in for Miss Alston. I've recently come from the La Junta house in Colorado. The longer you are employed by the Harvey Company, the more you will experience the privilege of travel." Steel-gray eyes roamed over the crowd of girls.

"Be warned. Just because I'm a substitute, does not mean I don't demand the utmost respect. I can take away points as easily as Miss Alston can give them." She clapped her hands. "Away with you all. There's work to be done and little time to do it."

Katie headed to her usual morning station and got to work filling the large coffee urns. Sarah could take over once the doors opened, but it was better if they both started the day doing what they knew best. She scanned the room for her friend. Where was she? Katie couldn't do tables and counter. They'd be in trouble for sure.

The new head waitress glared when Katie's gaze met hers. She ducked her head and concentrated on the coffee. *Sarah, where are you?*

Several minutes later, Sarah barreled into the dining room, the bow on her apron crooked and hair flying loose from its pins. Katie rushed to her side and helped get her back to standard. "Where have you been?"

"I overslept."

"I woke you almost an hour ago." Katie yanked the bow tight.

"I fell back to sleep. Don't nag. I didn't sleep well last night after my ordeal."

Remorse left a sour taste in Katie's mouth. "I'm sorry. You're right, but the new head waitress is extremely stern, and I don't—"

"Get to work, ladies. The doors are opening." Miss Dunlap glided past them.

Sarah gripped Katie's hands. "Thank you so much for trading places."

"You're welcome." Katie scurried to her assigned table and plastered a smile to her face. "Welcome. How may I serve you?" she said to two men in business suits. From the corner of her eye, she spotted Amos sidling his way to his usual place, casting glances Katie's way.

"Coffee for both of us," one of them said. "We'll also have the corned beef hash, O'Brien."

Katie headed to the kitchen to place the food order.

As she headed to her next table, she spotted Sarah giggling at something Amos said. Hurt back indeed! Katie hoped she wouldn't give her stepfather too much information about Katie's habits.

By the time she delivered the next table's orders of omelets, the food for the first table was finished. Katie hefted the heavy tray and pushed through the kitchen's swinging door. Waiting the tables made the morning fly by much faster than working the counter. She spotted Ward entering the room and taking his usual stool. Not being able to wait on him was the downside to switching places. She needed to spend regular time with him in order for him to see she wasn't a hardened criminal. She refused to acknowledge that spending time with him was also very pleasant. She needed to concentrate on her job and clearing her name, not on how a handsome man's attentions made her feel.

Her foot caught on the rung of a chair as Amos scooted his stool back. Katie did some fancy footwork, but lost the battle. The tray slipped from her hands and dumped hash down his back.

He leaped to his feet. "Again? Seriously, girl. You're a menace."

Tears stung her eyes. She hated the man but really hadn't intended to spill another person's breakfast on him. "I'm sorry, it's only that—"

"Miss Gamble, please escort me to the kitchen while the busboys clean up your mess. Sir, your meal is on the house."

Katie followed Miss Dunlap, feeling very much like a wayward school child.

The moment they entered the kitchen, the head waitress faced Katie with a glare. "I know that Miss Alston has nothing but high thoughts of you, but that gentleman complained to me earlier that you seem to have a personal vendetta against him. It seems he may be correct." She arched a brow.

"No, ma'am. I tripped when he scooted backward. I'm a good worker, honest." Katie refused to cower in front of the woman.

"You don't usually work the tables, do you?"

"No, ma'am."

Miss Dunlap nodded. "You will continue to do so. You are sadly lacking in your training. I will take the matter upon myself and see that you are up to Harvey standards by the time I leave. Please serve your customers a fresh meal."

Katie expelled a deep breath and sagged against the kitchen counter. The head waitress may view waiting on tables as a punishment, but to Katie it was an easier means to stay away from Amos. She'd ask one of the other girls if she could trade stations with them, thus putting her two tables farther away from the lunch counter.

"What a beast." Rachel carried in an empty tray. "You'd best get out there and see if your tables need anything else. If they don't, then roll silverware. Anything to look busy, or that woman will have your head."

"Thank you for the warning, but I've experienced her bite firsthand." Katie straightened. The chef handed her two plates of hash. Squaring her shoulders, Katie headed back to the guillotine.

Ward sipped his coffee and listened as Amos complained to Sarah and anyone else who would listen about the poor service and work ethic Katie had. His hand trembled as he replaced the cup on the saucer, causing the two to clink together. Only his strict guidelines in keeping control of himself as befitting the badge in his pocket kept him from throttling the man.

Sarah didn't seem to be suffering from her ordeal of the night before. Instead, she flirted with every male customer regardless of the man's age. Had she learned nothing? Ward sighed and turned his attention to the dining area.

The head waitress stood with beady eyes focused on the girls as a crow would be on a choice insect. He slid from his stool, motioned for Sarah to refill his coffee, then made his way to the head waitress's side. "Ma'am."

Her lips thinned in a smile. "Is everything to your liking, sir?"

"Very much. I wanted to let you know that Miss Gamble is an impeccable waitress. Mr. Moore goads her into reacting unfavorably. I hope you won't hold this morning's episode too strongly against her."

The woman stood as if she had a tree trunk down the back of her blouse. "Pardon me, sir, but we have a certain standard to uphold and can't let every man who is influenced by a pretty face cause us to lower those standards. Miss Gamble made a mistake, pure and simple."

Ward almost flashed the woman his badge to show her he wasn't just a man influenced by a pretty face. Instead, he kept a smile on his face, despite the woman's sour attitude. "You have a good day, ma'am, and keep up the good work." He couldn't return to his stool fast enough. The head waitress sent chills down his spine.

"Thank you, but not necessary," Katie said as she passed.

So, she'd noticed his attempt to placate her temporary boss. The thought warmed him more than the coffee. He lifted his mug. It didn't hurt to keep the feisty, alleged crook on his good side.

He stared into the dark brew in his hand. The more he got to know Katie, the more he hoped she wasn't guilty. It would break his heart to have to arrest her.

She carried a weapon and wasn't afraid to use said weapon. She had a beautiful face, but step on her wrong side, or threaten someone she cared about, and you'd see the rattlesnake side. Possessing a gun wasn't a sign of wrongdoing. It could be nothing more than a single woman wanting to protect herself. Ward shook his head, clearly in a dilemma. He'd never had such trouble determining someone's guilt—or innocence—before. Maybe Miss Dunlap was right and he was swayed by a pretty face.

"You're a Ranger, right?" Amos swiveled on his stool.

"Yes." Ward set his cup back on the saucer.

"Then why ain't you arresting that gal?"

"What do you know about it?"

"I'm the one who alerted the authorities." He crossed his arms.

"You don't say." Ward pretended to be more concerned with his drink than in what the other man had to say.

"Yep. She stole money and a deed from me. A deed left to me by my late wife. The dearest woman God ever put on this earth." Amos swiped a finger under a dry eye.

Ward wasn't fooled. The more the man kept talking, the less he was inclined to believe a word he said. Still, the lack of evidence on either side would keep him in Somerville for another week or so. "Rest assured that I'm looking into things." He cut the man a stern glance. "Both sides of the disagreement."

"You don't say." Amos tossed his words back to him. "That's good to know." He slid from the stool and marched outside.

Ward paid for his coffee and followed Amos. With breakfast over, he made a beeline for the nearest saloon. Ward shook his head. He didn't want to frequent the saloon to keep an eye on the man. Besides, Amos would be alerted now. Katie was the best hope Ward had at getting to the bottom of things. He'd have to watch for the right opportunity to ask her outright about the accusations.

A wagon rumbled down the street. Ward lifted his hand in greeting. Why wouldn't his family use the automobile?

"Good morning, son." Ma beamed down at him. "Your pa is treating me to a fancy meal in the restaurant. Said it was better to do so when Caroline wasn't around so she wouldn't be embarrassed by us."

"She would never be embarrassed." Ward reached up to help his mother down.

"I was only joshin'," Pa said, holding out a hand to Lucy. "Have you had breakfast yet, son?"

"Just coffee."

"Then come on and join us. You know what's eatable here."

If she didn't think so already, Katie would definitely think Ward was stalking her. The moment they stepped inside, Lucy called out a greeting, drawing the attention of the head waitress from them to Katie, who cringed in spite of her smile.

"Act like a lady," Ma scolded. "Do not yell across a room."

Ward led them to an empty table and helped Ma into a chair. His family stared at the luxurious surroundings with wide eyes. Although Ma kept a good house, the family didn't dine on china plates and crisp white tablecloths with matching napkins. Ward enjoyed their expressions as if he owned the restaurant. Now, if he could only get them to accept the luxury of a motor-driven car.

"The food here is fancier than what Ma cooks, but not near as tasty." He spread his napkin in his lap. "The waitresses are as pleasant as they are lovely to look at."

"I can see why you spend so much time here," Pa said, studying the waitress who filled his coffee. "But I suspect there might be one in particular that draws you here. Which one is she?"

Ward's mouth dried up.

"That one." Lucy pointed at Katie. "Isn't she lovely?"

Ward's neck heated and he avoided the gazes of his parents. "It isn't like that. I'm here on assignment—"

"You're working?" Ma narrowed her eyes.

Ward was dead.

Chapter 9

"Are you going to the Harvest Festival?" Sarah asked, sticking the last hairpin into her up-do.

"I wasn't aware of it." Had Katie been so involved in proving her innocence to Ward and staying away from Amos that she'd missed something of importance?

"The town supposedly puts one on every year. It starts at four this afternoon. All the girls are going." Sarah winked in the mirror. "I intend to find my husband today."

Katie frowned. The other girl would never make it the length of her contract before dashing to the altar. She took one last glance in the mirror before grabbing her purse and Bible. "I'm glad it begins after church."

"You're so godly." Sarah gave her a quick hug. "I wish I were half as good."

If only Sarah knew the truth. Katie was anything but godly. She rushed from the room before the girl could say anything more that would heap spiritual coals on Katie's head. Despite her feeling as if God paid little attention to what she did, she hurried to church, sliding into a back pew. She clutched her Bible like a lifeline and stared at the simple wooden cross at the front of the church.

Godly? Katie Gamble? Hardly. She might not be the crook Amos tried to make her out to be, but she definitely wasn't as good as Sarah said. Blinking back tears, Katie ducked her head and tried to be invisible. Church was the one place she wouldn't run into Amos, but Ward was another story. He and his family never missed a Sunday.

"Good morning, Katie." Ward, surrounded by his family, smiled down at her. "My mother would like to issue you an invitation to supper some Sunday after church."

Why? Katie's breath caught. She'd be surrounded by Alstons, all wanting to know more about her. "Thank you, but I'll be attending the Harvest Festival this afternoon. I'll be serving…something." Now, she'd have to find someone to volunteer to.

"That's all right, dear." Mrs. Alston reached over and patted her hand. "I meant sometime in the future. We'll be at the festival, too. Maybe we'll bump into each other."

Katie nodded as if her tongue had been removed. Heat rushed up her neck and into her face. She was an idiot. Of course they hadn't meant that day. She wanted to melt into the seat and out of everyone's sight.

Their footsteps faded away as they moved toward the front of the church. Her mother's voice rang in her to sit up and pay attention to God's word. After peering from under her lashes to make sure no one was paying her too much attention, Katie straightened and tried to focus on the service.

After mouthing a few hymns, her off-key singing would only draw attention, Katie strained to hear the pastor speak on trusting God and letting go of the reins. Easier said than done. She doubted the pastor had ever found himself in the type of fix she was in. No, she would keep praying for protection. Getting Amos to leave her alone and for Ward to believe she wasn't a crook, those things were on her shoulders alone. God had much bigger things to worry about than a mere girl trying to hold on to her land.

As soon as the last amen was spoken, she slid from her seat and bolted from the church. Outside, she stood off to the side until she spotted the pastor's wife make her way to the empty lot beside the church.

"Mrs. Logan." Katie rushed after her.

The woman turned, a smile gracing her round face. "May I help you?"

"I've learned there is a festival this afternoon and I'd like to volunteer my services."

"How wonderful." Mrs. Logan clapped her hands. "Can you be here by three-thirty? I can set you up at the lemonade stand."

Katie nodded. Clutching her Bible to her chest she made her way to the dormitory. She'd be working at the festival. Now, she could keep an eye on the partygoers while not having to engage herself. She had learned through the years that volunteer work was always the perfect excuse not to have to mingle.

After whiling away the next couple of hours over a leisurely lunch at the diner, and keeping an eye on the street for any signs of Amos, Katie reported to the pastor's wife at three-thirty sharp.

"Bless you, child." Mrs. Logan took her hands. "What is your name?"

Katie shifted under her kind scrutiny and slowly pulled her hands free, pretending to search for something in her purse. "Katie Gamble, ma'am. I'm a Harvey Girl at the hotel."

"Wonderful. We've borrowed the large pots for coffee and several pitchers for lemonade from there. I'm putting you in charge of the drink station. All drinks are a nickel."

She laughed, the sound soft and pleasing. "You'll be busier than a lone bee in a garden."

Katie returned the woman's smile and followed her to a horseshoe of tables set up as a counter. This she could do. She was volunteering in an area she had expertise in. Without further coaching, she got to work making coffee and assigned a young girl, Janie, who was also volunteering, to squeeze the lemons.

A deep laugh drew her attention, and she glanced over the coffee urn to see Ward marking off a horseshoe pit. His muscles rippled under the flannel shirt he wore as he lined up his shot and tossed the horseshoe. It fell around its target with a sharp metallic clamor. He glanced up and grinned when he saw her watching. Katie gasped and withdrew back around the urn that, when placed on the table, was as tall as she.

"Isn't he a dream?" Janie sighed. "If he's still available once I hit eighteen, I plan to set my cap for him."

"He is a handsome man." No sense in Katie denying she thought so. All the waitresses drooled when Ward walked in.

"Who's handsome?"

Katie whirled to see Ward grinning down at them. She dropped the carafe she had poured some of the coffee into, spilling hot coffee down the front of her dress.

Ward leaped over the table when Katie cried out. "I'm so sorry for startling you." He grabbed a handful of napkins and dabbed at her front.

"Stop." Her face reddened, whether from embarrassment or pain, he wasn't sure.

"Are you burned?" He quickly untied her apron and plucked it away from her.

"You're too familiar, Mr. Alston." Katie shoved him away from her. Her eyes glittered.

Was she crying? What a heel he was. "I'm sorry. Having sisters, I didn't think—" He hadn't meant to overstep any boundaries. Fearing she had just filled the carafe, he hadn't thought of anything but keeping her from injury.

"I'm fine." She pulled the apron over her head and wadded it into a ball. "You reacted so quickly, the coffee barely made it through the thick canvas of the apron. For that, I thank you."

"May I get you anything? Are there more aprons? Would you like me to take over your station?" He couldn't care less that he didn't act like a Texas Ranger at that moment. All he cared about was undoing the harm he'd done. If his fellow Rangers could see him, he'd be the butt of their jokes for weeks.

"I suppose you could make the coffee and lemonade, and I could oversee the horseshoes." A dimple winked next to her rosy lips. "But I don't really know anything about the game."

Ward suddenly couldn't take his eyes off her mouth. What would it be like to kiss her? Would she taste as sweet as she looked?

"Ward?"

"Huh?" He yanked his attention away from lips that had curled into a beguiling smile.

"I said I'm fine, and I'll send Janie for a clean apron." She crossed her arms.

"Oh, yes, all right." Ward walked around the table this time as the first customers of the festival arrived. "Yell if you need anything."

Idiot. He kicked at a rock as he made his way back to the horseshoe pit. He hoped that he'd be too busy manning the game to dwell on the lips of a raven-haired, dark-eyed, alleged crook.

He waved at Lucy, who strolled past with a group of giggling girls. Where were his parents? They rarely let their youngest child out of their sight. Maybe they figured she'd be safe in a group. It was good they were allowing her a bit of freedom. Wild-spirited Lucy wasn't created to be kept in a cage. He glanced at the drink stand, amused and envious that the line, mostly men, stretched a ways back. Mrs. Logan knew what she was doing by assigning drinks to two lovely women. Men and boys were apt to develop a thirst just for the opportunity to speak with them.

Ward was mighty thirsty himself. A glance at his watch showed his shift was over in fifteen minutes. He'd make a lot of men mad when he cut to the front of the line, one of the advantages of being a volunteer.

When break time finally came around, Ward made his way to Katie's station. "Lemonade, please. Don't you ladies get a break?"

Katie handed him a tall glass. "My shift is over in thirty minutes."

"May I buy you a cotton candy?"

Her eyes lit up. "I've never had one. That would be a delight."

"Go on along now, Katie." Mrs. Logan stepped up and tied an apron around her waist. "You young people go enjoy the festival."

Soon, Ward strolled the normally vacant field with the prettiest girl in town. She sighed with delight at her first taste of the spun candy, and Ward promised to win her the biggest prize at the festival.

"How strong are you?" Katie stuck a bite of candy in her mouth, sucking the sugar from her finger.

Ward's heart stopped, and his mind veered off into dangerous directions. He might not be strong enough to resist her charm. "Physically?"

"What else, silly man?"

"Strong enough." He flexed his muscles and got in line to hit a rubber baffle with a huge hammer and ring a bell.

Prize was a pig. What in the world would Katie do with a piglet? Nevertheless, he intended to win the squealing little critter for her, then he intended to take her on the new carousel. He could seat her on a wooden horse and wrap his arms around her waist in the pretense of keeping her from falling off.

When it was his turn, he handed over the quarter for three tries. He hefted the heavy hammer, raised it over his head, and lowered it with all his might. The painted arrow rose two-thirds of the way. His second try rose a bit higher. Closing his eyes, he focused all his strength on his last hit. Bong!

Katie clapped. "I've got a pig!"

Ward laughed and grabbed the frantic animal. "What are you going to do with her?"

"Give her to Lucy. I just wanted to see whether you were as strong as you said you were."

"You, Miss Gamble, are a regular tease." He handed the piglet back to the man with the promise to return at the end of the festival and collect her. "Carousel?"

"I'd be delighted." Katie slipped her arm through Ward's.

He wished with all his might that she was enjoying herself as much as he was. That for the afternoon, they no longer played a game of cat and mouse. No, for that day, they were a courting couple, intent on enjoying as much of the festival as possible.

When Ward lifted Katie onto a white horse, then stood with one arm around her waist, knowing she didn't need him to keep her stable, but not stepping back anyway, he knew the time had come for a serious conversation with his boss. Ward might no longer be the wisest choice to investigate the lovely Katie Gamble.

Chapter 10

Katie hid in the pantry and closed her eyes. Why couldn't every day be as wonderful as the one before? Yesterday, she'd served the folks of her new home and spent the afternoon with an attractive, attentive man who made her feel as if she were the most beautiful woman in the state of Texas. Unfortunately, dreams came to an end. Today, it was back to work and back to reality. She could never have a relationship with Ward Alston. Not until she resolved the problem of Amos and her land and cleared her name.

"Miss Gamble."

Katie opened her eyes. A stern Miss Dunlap glared at her with arms crossed. Oh, when would Miss Alston return? "Ma'am?"

"Why, exactly, are you napping in the pantry? Our breakfast guests are arriving."

Katie scampered past her like a mouse running from a cat. She grabbed a basket of rolled silverware from the counter on her dash to the restaurant. Why did the woman always catch her dawdling? That wasn't Katie's way, yet the few times she wasn't working, the woman caught her. That was what happened when a foolish girl dreamed of things that couldn't be.

"Good morning. How may I serve you?" Her first customers were a family of four. A man with his face buried in the morning paper and a harried woman with two children under the age of three.

"Thank you, miss." The woman gave a tired smile. "We've had a long journey by train and still have a ways to go, although it is nice not to have to cook. We'll have two orders of eggs and bacon with toast and milk for the little ones."

One of the best aspects of being a Harvey waitress was serving others. Moments like those helped shove the unpleasant times to the back of her mind. "I'll have that for you right away." Katie scurried to the next table, where two men in suits ordered coffee and the egg breakfast.

With a smile on her face, Katie headed to the kitchen and placed the orders. Since eggs were the regular morning meal for that day, the meal was prepared in record time, further adding to the tired mother's pleasure. Even Amos's scowl from the counter couldn't dispel the joy Katie received in lessening someone else's burden. Although she did spare a moment to wish the man would fall into a deep hole.

"Have you seen Sarah?" Rachel asked as she passed, balancing a large tray.

Katie shook her head. "She woke before I did."

"That girl is so starry-eyed about catching a husband, she's going to be fired." Rachel lowered her voice. "Especially if the new dragon of a head waitress finds out she isn't at her post."

Katie glanced at the counter, where a girl she didn't recognize poured coffee. "Maybe she's ill?"

"Not likely." Rachel continued on her way and deposited plates of food in front of her customers.

It might not be any of her business, but Katie couldn't help but feel responsible for her flighty roommate. After making sure her customers were taken care of, she moved through the kitchen and out the back door of the restaurant.

Sarah leaned against a tree and giggled with a young man in denim pants and a flannel shirt. Katie marched toward them. "Get back to your post."

Sarah sighed. "I will, but I don't see the use. Wilbur and I are going to be married."

The young man blushed. "Work as long as possible, sweetheart. We'll need the money to buy our own farm."

Sarah rose on tiptoe and planted a kiss on the man's cheek. "One month. That's all I'll give you." With a flirty wave, she dashed back to the restaurant, leaving Katie to follow.

Miss Dunlap waited for her just inside the door. "Meeting gentlemen during working hours? I am sorely disappointed. This is a mark against you, Miss Gamble."

"No, I… My apologies." Katie ducked her head and tried to scoot around her substitute boss. It wouldn't do any good to correct her. In doing so she'd only jeopardize her friend.

"I am not finished." Miss Dunlap lifted her chin. "As further discipline, I insist you work past quitting time and remove all the soiled tablecloths and take them to the laundry."

Katie's shoulders sagged. She was already exhausted at the end of each day. "Yes, ma'am."

"What is going on here?" Miss Alston set her tapestry bag on the floor and approached them. "Has Katie done something wrong?"

"You're early." Some of the starch went out of Miss

Dunlap's attitude. "This girl has been keeping company with men during work hours."

"Katie? Is it true?"

"No, ma'am. It's a misunderstanding."

"I saw her with my own eyes." Miss Dunlap crossed her arms.

"Thank you for your concern. I'll handle things from here. Katie is one of our best girls. I'm sure she did nothing wrong." Miss Alston gave the other woman a smile, clearly dismissing her. "Now, Katie, please explain."

Miss Dunlap huffed and headed out of the kitchen.

"I was looking for one of the other girls, and Miss Dunlap caught me reentering the kitchen."

"Someone else was slacking on the job?"

"I'd rather not say, ma'am. She's back at work now with no harm done." She hoped Miss Alston wouldn't make her say the name. She had so few friends.

Miss Alston pressed her lips together and tapped them with her forefinger. "I understand your loyalty, Katie, but sometimes, we have to spill the beans. Please let your friend know that while I strive to be fair, I cannot tolerate slacking."

Relief flooded Katie like water over a dam. "Thank you very much. I'll let her know."

She fairly skipped out of the kitchen and into Ward's arms.

"Whoa, easy now." Ward caught Katie before she sent them both tumbling to the ground. "Where's the fire?"

The fire was sweeping across her face. Being in his arms felt wonderful, but unseemly. She took two steps back. "Thank you for catching me. I must get back to work."

"The pleasure was all mine." He watched her scurry away, wishing she hadn't been in such a hurry to escape his hold. As dangerous as it might be, she felt as if she were made for him to hold. But she was something he could never have. He glanced at the telegram in his hand.

His boss had replied to one Ward had sent earlier by telling him to keep his emotions out of the investigation and to keep his mind on his job. He shook his head and shoved the slip of paper into the pocket of his denim pants. Only time would tell whether he could pursue a relationship with Katie.

"Thank you again for picking me up at the train station, although you know very well I could have walked. It's right across the street." Caroline exited the kitchen, her arms full of starched linens.

"You know Ma didn't want you to go straight back to work. She says you work too hard. Besides, meeting you at the station gave me an opportunity to walk with you."

Caroline raised her eyebrows and tapped him on the nose with a napkin. "You're smitten."

"I am not." His neck heated. "She's a suspect."

"Right."

"She is." A beautiful one. A woman he enjoyed spending time with. A woman who couldn't be anything more at that point.

"I'm inviting her to Sunday dinner."

"Ma already did."

"Really?"

"For sometime in the future. No date was set." How in the world would Ward get through a dinner with Katie sitting across the table? "She's still a bit skittish around me. We should wait a week or two." He would draw out the investigation as long as possible and use the time to get to know her better. Then, if he proved her innocence, he could ask to actively court her without pretense—after he apologized profusely for doubting her in the first place.

"Do you need coffee?"

His sister's question drew him back to the present. "No, thank you. I had more than enough cups at home. Ma seems to want to fill me with anything she can, whether food or drink."

"She loves having you home."

Ward loving being home, but he if didn't have a job to do, he'd be going nuts from boredom. "I'll see you later. Coming by after work?"

"I'll try." She patted his face and slid the linens under the lunch counter.

Having left his sister happily ensconced in her job, Ward left the restaurant to get started on the next step of his investigating plan. He wanted to check out the boardinghouse where Amos resided while in Somerville. The proprietress, Mrs. Jackson, would tell him what he wanted to know. After all, she'd been friends with Ma since they'd attended school together.

He stepped into the midmorning sun and frowned. His automobile sported a flat tire. Where in Somerville could he find a replacement? The mercantile sold gasoline, but they didn't carry automobile parts. They could order him one, but that could take days, and he hated to leave his new beauty on the street for that length of time.

He knelt beside the Ford and spotted a two-inch slit in the tire. Someone had decided to divert him from his plans for the day, and a cut of that type could only be made with a knife. He straightened and studied the street.

There was very little traffic, foot or otherwise, at that time of day. A couple of elderly men played checkers in front of the mercantile, and from the direction of the school came the sounds of students at recess. When the train arrived in an hour for the lunch crowd, the street would be teeming with passengers. Other than that, no one seemed overly interested in Ward.

Should he tell the sheriff, or investigate the vandalism on his own? Since he had no clues to go on, he decided to see what he could find on his own. But first, he'd need help getting the automobile off the streets.

He headed to the livery, where he could hopefully get a couple of willing hands to help push the car. "Howdy, Wilbur. Got a minute?"

The young man straightened from where he studied the foot of a horse. "Sure. What do you need?"

"Help pushing my Ford here? I've got a flat."

Wilbur laughed. "You seem to have a lot of trouble with that conveyance. Ought to stick to a horse."

"Then I'd just throw a shoe."

"True, and they eat a lot. Once all the kinks are worked out of automobiles, I intend to get me one. Me and my girl."

"Got your eye on someone?" Ward asked as they made their way to his car.

"Sarah, the prettiest Harvey Girl in the state."

Ward could argue with that, but he'd let the starry-eyed young man dwell on his dreams. "Know anywhere I can get a spare?"

"Sure." Wilbur placed his shoulder along the passenger-side door. "We started carrying them a few weeks ago. Seems more and more people are buying these things. I can have you fixed up within the hour."

"That's wonderful." That left Ward plenty of time to find out what he could about Amos Moore.

As they pushed, Amos strolled out of the saloon and shaded his eyes. Spotting Ward and Wilbur pushing the car down the rutted main street, he laughed. "Got trouble, boys?"

"We could use another hand, if you're willing." Ward narrowed his eyes.

"Not willing." The man gave a nod and headed in the other direction, his laugh still ringing across the morning.

Chapter 11

While his tire was being replaced, Ward continued on his quest to find out more about Amos Moore. Instinct told him the man wasn't an upstanding citizen and that he was in Somerville for a reason other than to see Katie prosecuted. Everyone Ward had spoken to so far, albeit regular visitors to the saloon, said Amos was nothing but a good ole boy out for some fun.

Somehow, he needed to find out Katie's side of the story in depth. The real story. Ward was used to hardened criminals. Not beautiful women with starlit eyes.

The boardinghouse sat at the end of the street close to the church. Ward marched up the steps and rapped the lion's head–shaped knocker against the door.

The door swung open, answered by Mrs. Jackson. "Mr. Alston, welcome." She stood back and waved him inside. "Would you like a glass of lemonade? I know you aren't looking for a room, so it must be information you're after."

"Yes, to both, ma'am, and I think we've known each

other long enough that you can call me Ward." He followed her into the kitchen, where the aroma of cinnamon and apples filled the room. Next to his mother's home cooking, he preferred that of his mother's lifelong friend.

"Sit and tell me what's on your mind." She fetched two glasses from a cabinet and filled them with lemonade.

"It's about one of your boarders."

"Oh, dear. I hope I'm not harboring a fugitive." Her hand fluttered at the lace around her throat.

"That's what I'm trying to find out."

She sat his glass in front of him and took a seat to his right. "Well, goodness. Don't keep me in suspense."

Ward took a sip of the sweet tart drink and wiped his mouth on the back of his hand. "It's about Amos Moore."

She wrinkled her nose. "*Smarmy* is the only word to describe that man. He comes across as fine as flour, but you can see in his eyes that something ain't right."

"How so?" He sure had a hankering for the apple Betty he smelled. His stomach rumbled.

"Let me get you some of that dessert first." She grinned.

Two minutes later, he had a hot plate of apple Betty in front of him. "I didn't take this out of the mouths of your boarders, did I?"

She waved away his words. "I've plenty." She leaned her elbows on the table and lowered her voice. "The only thing of any importance I can tell you is that the man boasts constantly about coming into a bunch of money. Said he's taking somebody down and moving on. Does that make sense to you?"

"Quite a bit actually." The delicious treat lost some of its sweetness. He'd bet his Ford that Katie was the one Amos intended to take down. "You be careful around him."

"He don't bother me. Comes and goes, rarely even eats here." She set her glass on the washboard. "You think of anything else you want to know, come see me. I'll keep my ears and eyes wide-open."

"Thank you, Mrs. Jackson."

"You tell your Ma howdy for me and that we are long overdue for some girl time."

He grinned and pushed his chair back. "I sure will."

The dessert filled the empty spot in his belly. He'd be good until supper now. Back outside, he tugged his hat low against the brilliant sunlight and scanned the street.

The train roared into the station with smoke and whistle. Ward headed that way, hoping there would be someone getting off who might shed some light on the mystery he found himself in. Something, anything, that would help him put this case to rest.

He stood under the station roof's overhang and did his best to appear as a casual observer, blending into the shadows. He'd learned a long time ago how easy it was to go unnoticed when he wanted to. He leaned against the warm brick, bent his leg, resting the bottom of his boot against the building, and slouched.

Soon, the platform swarmed with people. One wide-eyed girl could possibly be a new Harvey waitress. Ward straightened when a petite brunette in a modern spotless canary-yellow dress stepped from the train. A large feather-plumed hat shaded her face. She moved as if she knew where she was going and disappeared in the throng of people. Following close behind were three men in rough clothes and dusty boots. Cowhands, maybe. Other than those four, no one caught his attention. He'd wasted half an hour on a hopeful ruse for clues.

He headed to the telegraph office to send a message regarding the information Mrs. Jackson had told him. If nothing else, it might get him a respite from his boss's daily demands to know when things would be wrapped up in Somerville. If Ward didn't find concrete evidence of

Katie's guilt or innocence, he feared there might be another Ranger sent to town to investigate and that Ward would be moved to another location. He couldn't let that happen.

"Afternoon, son." Pa pulled up in the buckboard. "Can I give you a lift somewhere?"

Ward pushed his hat out of his eyes. "No, thanks. Heading to the telegraph office, then to pick up my car. Had a flat this morning."

Pa chuckled. "Told you horses were better. See you at supper." He clicked his tongue and moved down the street.

When would people leave him alone about his Ford? He loved the automobile. They were the future. Soon enough, everyone in town would own one. He continued his march down the sidewalk and shoved through the door of the telegraph office. After sending his message, he stepped back outside just in time to see Katie dart across the street in her work uniform and disappear inside the mercantile.

"Afternoon, Katie." The owner's sister, Mrs. Meyer, greeted her with a smile. "On your break?"

"One of the few we get." Katie headed for the fabric. She so wanted a new frock. With money in her pocket, she could indulge once in a while, and now was one of those times. She needed to look the part of a woman with no worries if she wanted Ward to stop looking at her with suspicion. Despite his admiring glances, she knew the real reason he spent time with her. He had a job to do and would do it thoroughly, she was sure. A spark of hope leaped in her heart. During his investigation, Ward was bound to find out Katie wasn't the bad guy. Surely the truth would come out.

She ran her hand over a bolt of yellow linen. It would look wonderful made into a dress she'd seen in the Sears, Roebuck & Co. catalog. "I'll take this." She set the bolt on the counter. While Mrs. Meyer cut the right amount of fabric, Katie wandered the store.

A stack of posters hanging next to the post office window caught her eye and she flipped through them. An etched drawing of her face stared back at her. Wanted for questioning, Katie Gamble. With a glance to see whether she was being observed, she pulled the paper from the nail and folded it inside her purse. Her heart threatened to hammer out of her rib cage.

She flipped through more of the posters. Toward the bottom, she came across one like the one she'd found before fleeing her home. Now that she studied the picture, it looked an awful lot like Amos. Could he be a bank robber? She ripped it free and let the other pages flutter back into place.

Should she tell Ward of her suspicions, or would he only want to know why she felt compelled to look through wanted posters? The first time she'd glanced through them weeks ago, she'd found nothing to cause alarm. This time, the drawing of her face sent ice through her veins. Wanted posters weren't usually something that attracted a refined woman's attention, and twice she'd been drawn to them. She cupped her face. Oh, what should she do?

"Your fabric is cut," Mrs. Meyer said. "Is there anything else I can get you?"

"Some matching thread, please. And a packet of needles." Katie's hands shook as she dug the money from her purse. She needed to decide what to do about Amos's poster. What if she mentioned it to Ward and he started looking posters up somewhere else and found hers? Her stomach roiled. "Thank you." She grabbed the fabric wrapped in brown paper and rushed out the door.

Ward jumped out of her way. "We seem to meet a lot with you almost running me over."

"My apologies." She continued her mad dash down the sidewalk. "Can't talk now, I'm going to be late."

She leaped into the street, then jumped back with a shriek, narrowly being missed by a horse and buggy.

Ward grabbed her arm and pulled her back to the sidewalk. "Please allow me to escort you."

Obviously, she was incapable of crossing the street alone. She hung her head and clutched her fabric to her chest. Mortification burned her cheeks. Ward must think her a complete imbecile.

Their boots beat out a steady beat on the sidewalk as he walked her to the corner. With his hand burning through her dress to the small of her back, he guided her across the street and onto the porch of the restaurant.

"Be careful, Katie. You're much too lovely to be run over." He tipped his hat and set off.

The pounding of her heart after finding her picture on a wanted poster didn't come close to how it raced now. Goodness, she was in trouble.

She pushed open the door and headed to her room to stash her purchase in her bureau drawer. Working in the evenings and on Sunday afternoons, she could have the dress finished quickly and ready for the promised invitation to dine at the Alstons'. After checking her reflection in the mirror and poking some wayward strands of hair into place, she went back to the restaurant to prepare for the dinner rush.

"Don't think cozying up to that Ranger will keep the truth from coming out." Amos cornered her on the way to her tables. He pinched the delicate skin under her arm. "I'll have my day, missy." He leered and headed for the counter.

Katie rubbed her arm and glared before heading back to the kitchen. "Miss Alston?"

"Yes, Katie." The head waitress stepped out of the pantry.

"May I continue waiting the tables in place of Sarah? That one man continues to harass me."

"Shall I have the manager refuse him service?" Miss Alston's usually calm face appeared concerned.

"No, that's all right." Katie didn't want him accosting her on the street where there weren't witnesses. "I enjoy the tables and it will be harder for him to approach me."

"Very well. You may continue with the tables. I'll let Sarah know."

"Thank you." Katie scooted out of the kitchen just as the dinner crowd entered.

A lovely woman about her size, and resembling Katie enough that they could be sisters or maybe cousins, glided into the room wearing a lovely silk gown of lavender and took a seat at Katie's table. Katie squelched her desire for such fine clothing and went to take the woman's order.

"Yes, I'll have the salad and a glass of tea, please," the woman said. "And the steak. A big one."

"Yes, ma'am. My pleasure." Katie was surprised at the hard lines on the woman's face. Could she have pulled herself out of a harsh life and now was able to enjoy the finer things? If so, then there was hope for Katie. "Are you staying in town long?"

"A few weeks. It's rather a quaint place, isn't it? I've booked a room here at this hotel. It's lovely."

"And the service is remarkable." Katie smiled then headed over to hand the chef the woman's order.

"That's a fine-looking woman," the chef said. "Although she looks a bit down in the mouth, doesn't she?"

Katie shrugged. She'd never been prone to gossip and didn't intend to start now. "She's quite pretty." Once the chef filled the woman's plate, Katie pushed the door open with her hip, her hands full.

Sitting at the woman's table was Amos.

Chapter 12

Katie's heart lodged in her throat. Why couldn't Amos spend his days somewhere else? Must he continually stalk her? She had no intention of handing over the deed to her land, threats or not. Especially with the promise of oil under the surface. She didn't understand everything about the resource, but knew enough to know it was a valuable commodity.

She set the woman's plate in front of her and glared at Amos. "How may I serve you?"

He sneered. "I'll have what my lady friend is having."

If the woman was a friend of Amos's, Katie's admiration for her dropped several notches. "I'll be right back."

"Don't bother." The woman spread her napkin in her lap. "We aren't friends, and this man is leaving." She pierced Amos with dark eyes.

He shrugged. "If you say so. I'm not hungry anyway." He stood and with a nod at Katie and the other lady, strolled out of the restaurant.

Katie watched him leave, made sure her customer was cared for, and then headed to the kitchen. What was wrong with that man? The wanted posters crinkled from the safety of her hidden pocket. If she kept adding stuff she wanted to keep secret, she'd have a noticeable lump on her hip very soon.

The clock showed an hour until her shift was up. Her steps lightened. It had been days since she'd had the time to take her evening stroll. She'd walk for a while then get started cutting out her new dress.

Keeping busy, she refilled the water pitchers, checked on her customers one more time, offering them chocolate cake for dessert, then untied her apron and tossed it in a bin of dirty laundry. The evening air beckoned, and she rushed outside, not changing from her uniform.

A breeze rustled the tree branches as she made her way to her favorite spot beside the creek. Since Miss Alston had mentioned going home for supper, Katie knew Ward wouldn't disturb her solitude that evening. She perched on a boulder and tossed pebbles into the water, the ripples smoothing away her stress as they disappeared along the shoreline.

She took the papers out of her pocket, still undecided as to what to do. A gust of wind made the decision for her, ripping them from her hands and fluttering them to the water's surface. Katie made a beeline for them, only managing to grab the one of Amos. The poster of her face smeared and the ink dissolved as it traveled downstream.

Hitching her skirt, she dashed along the shoreline until the paper wedged under thick brush sticking out into the water. Hopefully, no one would find it before the water completely tore it apart. She shook the poster of Amos and grimaced. His features were faint, along with the name, Burt Kilroy.

She slumped back on her rock seat and rested her chin in her hands. Tears pricked her eyes. She'd made a royal mess of things. So big, she had no idea how to repair the circumstances she found herself in. Peace broken, she headed in the direction of the dormitory. It was time to come clean with Ward. She'd show him the poster and seek his guidance. Maybe the sheet of paper was all she needed to have Amos put away once and for all.

Three men suddenly blocked her path. Her heart pounded. Taking a right, she dashed down another path, fumbling with her skirts to reach for her gun. Heavy footsteps and ribald comments chased her.

She turned again, trying to find a path back to the safety of the hotel. Her hearted sounded loud in her ears, her breathing labored. *Help me, God.* Pistol in hand, she came against an impenetrable stand of bushes. Hair in her face, she turned to face her pursuers.

"What do you want? I don't have any money." She aimed her pistol at the man in the middle.

"It ain't often we find such a pretty thing all alone in the woods." He stroked his heavy beard. Full lips pulled back from tobacco-stained teeth. "Of course, we didn't think she'd have claws."

"You have no idea. Now turn around and leave the way you came." Katie forced her hand to remain steady.

"Boss said we was to scare you real good." The man continued grinning while the other two goons leered silently. "You scared?"

"Not a bit." *Please don't let them see through my lie.*

"Maybe we should try harder." He motioned for one of the other men to step forward.

Katie pulled the trigger. The bullet kicked up dirt at the man's feet. "I won't miss next time." She smiled. "Are you scared?"

"Man, I didn't sign up for this," one of the men said. "We ain't even getting paid and I don't aim to get shot today. I'm leaving."

Three glares were sent Katie's way, leaving her trembling and shaking against a tree as they left. She swiped her sleeve across her eyes, wiping away tears. Keeping her gun in her hand, she continued her trek to the hotel, not putting the pistol away until the building loomed in sight.

She smoothed her dress and hair, not wanting anyone to see her frazzled and ask questions. What she wouldn't give for someone to talk to about her ordeal, to spill her fear to a man who wanted to protect her.

Tears started fresh and she thundered up the stairs, past the common room and into her bedroom, where thankfully, Sarah was absent. Katie threw herself on her bed and let the tears flow.

Was it wrong to want love? Was it wrong to want to hold on to what belonged to her? She rolled over onto her back and stared at the ceiling. Ward's face swam across the painted boards.

She wanted someone kind, compassionate and strong. Someone like Ward.

Ward exhaled and rubbed his stomach. "That was good eating, Ma."

"I hope you saved room for pie." She set a slice of apple pie in front of him and a large glass of milk. "You're nothing but skin and bones. Working yourself to death when you should be resting."

"My wound is healed." Ward picked up his fork and took a bite of apple goodness. The tart taste of the apple and the sweetness of the brown sugar melded together in perfect harmony.

"I think our dear brother is sticking around because of a certain raven-haired Harvey waitress." Caroline helped remove empty dishes from the table.

"Stop it." Ward pushed his plate away, not able to finish. "Sorry, Ma. I don't have an empty inch in my stomach."

"You've taken a liking to Katie?" Ma pushed the pie back in front of him.

Ward sighed and took another bite. "We're just friends." He'd get Caroline back somehow for her big mouth. Now, Ma would never leave him alone about bringing the girl over.

"You should invite her for supper after church next Sunday. It's time to set a definite date."

Ward groaned. While he wasn't averse to spending more time with Katie, he wasn't thrilled to do so under his mother's watchful eye and knowing smile. She'd be planning a wedding if he gave her even a small nudge. "I'll be leaving soon, Ma. Don't get too excited."

"You should settle down, help your father run the farm, have a family."

Someday, Ward intended to do that very thing. But that day wasn't today. He pushed back his chair. "I think I'll see if he needs my help in the barn."

"Run away." Caroline laughed.

He glared and hurried out the back door into the welcome peace of the cool evening. Cows lowed from the nearby pasture, adding their deep song to a cricket's serenade. Ward sat on the top step and studied the fertile land in front of him.

Pa had spent his entire life working the land handed down to him by his father. It was expected that someday Ward would take over. Not that Ward minded, but he loved being a Ranger. He liked helping to establish law and order in the state of Texas, but times were changing. More people were entering law enforcement. Maybe it was time for Ward to seriously think about sticking around Somerville.

It didn't take a lot of imagination to see a dark-haired wife and children who looked like her running around the farm. It was something to pray about at least. But first, he needed to unravel the mystery surrounding Katie. He wasn't sure his heart could take it if he found out she'd pulled the wool over his eyes.

Placing his hands on his knees, he pushed to his feet and headed for the barn. Pa had disappeared that way shortly after supper, and Ward knew he was sneaking in a smoke. Sure enough, he found him behind the barn, next to the toolshed.

"Doesn't Ma know you have your nightly pipe by now?" Ward leaned back against the horse paddock, leaning his arms behind him.

"She knows."

"Then why are you hiding?"

Pa grinned. "Because she doesn't like to let on that she knows. If she did, then people might think she condoned my one vice."

His parents had the type of marriage Ward wanted someday. One where they could be themselves and still be loved unconditionally. The way they loved their children, and the way God loved them all. He glanced overhead at the sky.

Stars too numerous to count blinked to life against a navy sky. Ward saw the same sky in his travels, but somehow it seemed bigger, brighter, in Somerville.

"Something on your mind, son?"

He wanted his father's advice, but didn't want to turn his opinion against Katie before he got to know her. "This case I'm on has so many twists and turns, I don't know which end is up."

"Have you asked the Lord to help you?" Pa blew a smoke ring. It shimmered gray in the night before thinning.

"No, I haven't." Ward looked at the case as his job, not God's. But maybe Pa was right. It wouldn't hurt to have some divine intervention.

"Do you spend so much time at the restaurant because

that pretty little gal is involved?" Pa tilted his head, peering through his smoke at Ward.

"Did Caroline say something?" Ward would throttle the blabbermouth.

"No, but all this talk about a pretty gal and work…well, it isn't too hard to put the pieces together. She's involved somehow and you don't like it a bit. Am I right?"

Ward sighed. "You're right."

"All the more reason to take it to the Lord." Pa tapped his pipe against the bottom of his shoe. "Your ma got any of that pie left?"

"I'm sure she does."

Pa clapped him on the shoulder. "Keep me company while I eat."

"Why don't you have dessert with the rest of us?"

"I've always had my smoke right after supper. I don't see a reason to change now."

"If you don't mind, I'll stay out here and walk around the place. Maybe it will clear my head."

"Good luck, son." Pa stomped the dirt from his boots and entered the kitchen.

Ward watched through the window as Pa placed a kiss on Ma's neck and she swatted him with a dish towel. He grinned at the familiar sight, even as his heart dropped. He'd never felt so lonely in his life.

His steps carried him into the barn where the horses were stabled for the night. He petted the nose of an ebony mare that reminded him of Katie's hair. Was Katie's hair as silky soft as the horse's muzzle? If he were to cup her cheek would she lean into his touch?

He shook his head. Those types of thoughts were good for nothing but keeping him awake at night. Until he solved the case, he couldn't fantasize about a relationship of any kind with any woman, even Katie.

Chapter 13

Katie stepped into the bright afternoon sun after church and squinted against the glare. An empty Sunday afternoon loomed in front of her. She'd have hours on which to work on her new gown.

"There she is. Miss Gamble?" Ward's mother bustled toward her. Ward stood a few feet away with an apologetic look on his face. "Since it seems I can't rely on my son to issue an invitation, I'd like to extend one myself. Will you do us the honor of coming for Sunday supper? My Lucy is quite taken with you."

Katie bit her lip. Why her? Of all the single women in Somerville, why pick Katie Gamble, suspected thief? She forced a smile, unable to say no to the woman's earnest invite. "I'd be delighted."

Mrs. Alston laughed. "Don't look as if you're going to the guillotine, dear. It's only supper." She linked her arm through Katie's and drew her toward a wagon. "We're a bit cramped, so I'll send you in the automobile with Ward. I hope that's all right."

Speechless, Katie nodded and eyed the metal contraption. Ward gave a gallant wave. "Your carriage awaits."

She eyed the buckboard, then with a sigh, swept her skirt aside and climbed onto the leather seat of the Ford. It was more comfortable than the wagon, but as soon as Ward cranked the engine, her heart leaped into her throat. How did someone control something without reins? She studied Ward's strong hands on the wheel. When he turned, and the car responded, Katie understood. Still, the ride was bumpy, and she was grateful for the cushioned seats. She kept a hold of a leather strap above her head and tried not to bite her tongue.

"Don't worry." Ward grinned. "I'll get us there safely. Soon, all the roads in Somerville will accommodate vehicles. Everyone will own one."

Not Katie. She preferred the back of a horse or her own two feet. "We're going awfully fast."

"Only fifteen miles per hour."

So fast! She gripped the handhold tighter and tried to concentrate on the scenery whipping past. Fields, stripped of their cotton, stretched on both sides, broken only by the occasional stand of thick trees. The land was so flat it seemed as if she could see from one side of Texas to the other.

"Does your family own a lot of land?"

"About five hundred acres. When I settle down, I'll have a bit of money to buy an adjoining chunk of acreage one of our neighbors is thinking about selling."

Her heart stuttered. "You're thinking about quitting your job as a Ranger?"

"Not immediately, but someday." He turned them down a fairly smooth road and stopped in front of a two-story house with a sprawling front porch and several outbuildings.

His home made the small one-bedroom cabin she'd grown up in look like nothing more than a hillbilly shack. Maybe that was all it was, but the place was home. At least until Amos had moved in.

Ward cut the ignition then came around to her side to help her from the car. Her hand disappeared in his large one. She could have used his strength a few days ago when the men had accosted her in the woods. If she hadn't been alone, they wouldn't have dared, and she'd not gone to her favorite place since. She wasn't sure which made her angrier: the loss of her place of sanctuary, or the fact she'd had to draw her gun. This wasn't the Wild West. They lived in the twentieth century.

"Come on." Ward tugged on her hand. "Ma will be beside herself making sure everything is perfect. She knew you'd say yes."

"How could she possibly have known that?" She wanted to pull her hand free in order not to give his family the wrong idea, but Ward held tight.

He dragged her up the steps and through the front door. "You can hang your shawl there and deposit your purse on the side table if you'd like. We eat in the dining room on Sundays."

She smoothed the skirt of her peacock-blue dress. At least she'd worn one of her best that day. She still thought often of the lavender one worn by the woman who had sat at one of her tables, but new dresses were few and far between. Someday, Katie intended to move farther west, and her money needed to be saved.

Being led into the kitchen didn't leave a lot of time for Katie to gawk at her surroundings. Comfortable, sturdy furniture filled the room. Colorful rag rugs lay on the polished floors. Crocheted afghans draped over the arms of chairs. Not ritzy by any standards, but pleasant and wel-coming, from what she had time to see.

"You made it." Mrs. Alston turned with a grin. Lucy's face beamed from where she tossed hot rolls into a napkin-covered basket.

"What can I do to help?" Katie reached for an apron hanging on a hook.

"Nothing, of course." Mrs. Alston moved the apron out of her reach. "You're our guest. Go on into the dining room and talk with Mr. Alston and Ward. We'll be eating in a matter of minutes."

Katie wasn't one for small talk. In fact, having nothing to do but converse left her mouth dry. Nevertheless, she allowed Ward to lead her into the dining room.

"They were holding hands!" Lucy's shriek drifted her way. "I saw them through the window."

Katie's eyes widened and her face heated. She cupped her cheeks in an effort to cool them and met Ward's amused gaze.

"Don't listen to her. She looks for drama and romance under every rock." He pulled out a chair for her to sit down. "Afternoon, Pa."

Mr. Alston glanced over the top of his newspaper. "Same to you. Good day, young lady. As my son said, don't listen to the two chickens cackling in the kitchen. They've nothing else to do but gossip, it seems."

Katie loved him already. She smiled and glanced back at Ward.

It took all his strength to pull his gaze away from Katie's glowing face and take his own seat across the table from her. Pa had gone back to his newspaper. De-spite Ma's constant attempts to civilize him, he had yet to master social graces. Katie didn't seem to mind. She fiddled with her silverware and peered at Ward under lowered lashes.

"Ain't nothing new happening in the world today. At least nothing that concerns me, although the town over had its bank robbed. It's only a matter of time before it happens here." Pa rattled the paper as he refolded it. "How do you like your job at that fancy hotel and restaurant?"

"I like it fine. It's a lot of work, but the girls are pleasant enough, and your daughter is a joy to work under."

Pa flashed a grin. "You let me know if she gets too big for her britches."

Katie giggled. "I will, sir, and thank you."

"Here we are." Ma and Lucy carried in the fixings for a roast beef dinner. Biscuits, mashed potatoes, gravy and candied carrots completed the meal. She'd gone all out for their meal, and Ward could see the attempts at matchmaking she couldn't hide. "I hope you didn't talk of anything interesting while we were gone."

"No, ma'am." Ward stood and pulled out a chair for his mother. "We wouldn't dare." He winked at Katie, pleased at the way her cheeks darkened.

"That's a lovely dress, dear." Ma sat across from Pa. "May we call you Katie?"

"Please." Katie took a biscuit from the offered basket and passed it along. "Thank you. I purchased the loveliest yellow fabric the other day to make a new one. I had planned on finishing it today, but coming here is much nicer."

She couldn't have said anything better. Ma's grin stretched from ear to ear, and Ward's estimation of Katie grew a notch. He slopped a big spoonful of potatoes next to his meat and passed the bowl. "Ma's gravy is the best in the state."

"Oh, go on now." Ma waved his comment aside. "Do you cook, Katie?"

"My Ma always did the cooking, although I've done a bit here and there." Her smiled faded.

"Is she gone?"

"Yes. As of last year."

Ma reached across the table and patted her hand. "I'm sorry. You must miss her very much."

Katie nodded and spread her napkin in her lap. With what Ward knew of Katie and Amos, he knew she didn't want to dwell on the topic of her family. "I think my driving scared our guest."

"I'm not surprised. Noisy things, those cars." Ma folded her hands. "Say the blessing, Pa."

After Pa's short and sweet and to-the-point blessing, the five of them dug in with gusto. Lucy was uncharacteristically quiet, obviously trying to come up with the perfect question. "Katie, what do you do in your spare time?"

"I read some, do some mending and, until a few nights ago, I took leisurely strolls in the woods behind the restaurant."

"What happened?" Ward asked. What had caused her to quit something that brought her pleasure?

Katie's fork of potatoes halted halfway to her mouth. "Forget I said anything. It doesn't matter, and I'd hate to spoil the mood of this wonderful supper."

"What happened?" Ward narrowed his eyes.

She set her fork down. "Three men harassed me on my walk."

"Did they hurt you?" He'd hunt them down and watch them squirm before taking them to the sheriff.

"No, I handled it very well, thank you." She straightened her shoulders and met his gaze.

"What did you do?" Lucy asked breathlessly. "It sounds exciting."

"Hardly." Katie chuckled. "But I did pull my gun on

them and shot at their feet. They hurried off fast enough then."

Pa snorted and ducked his head. Ma sat with her mouth open, food forgotten. Lucy's eyes almost bugged out of her head, and Ward spewed his mouthful of milk. Wiping his mouth with his napkin, he asked. "You drew your gun on them? Are you crazy? What if they had been armed?"

"They weren't." She calmly took her bite of food. "I could see they weren't."

"I want to be you when I grow up." Lucy sighed. "You're beautiful *and* brave."

"Foolish is more like it." Ward tossed his napkin on the table and stood. "You could have been killed."

Katie shook her head. "I'm a very good shot. If you're that worried about me, then you should spend your energy trying to find out who hired them to scare me." She continued to eat as if she hadn't a care in the world. If not for the faint tremble of her hand, he would think the danger didn't concern her in the slightest.

"Settle down, son, and eat." Ma handed him back his napkin. "Katie seems to have handled the situation just as I would have."

"I'm surrounded by crazy women."

"Get used to it, son," Pa said. "They don't change, even after forty years of marriage."

He didn't want to get used to it. This whole situation just reinforced his idea he wasn't ready to settle down. He'd worry every minute over what danger his wife could get into. Especially one as feisty as Katie Gamble. He sat down and spread his napkin back in his lap.

"See, I told you I shouldn't have brought it up." Katie gave him a thin smile before buttering her biscuit. "You did insist."

"I did." He mumbled. "And I'm sorry for it."

She giggled, the sound as pleasant as the trickling of

water over rocks. "Don't ask any question you may not like the answer to."

"Well said." Ma clapped. "If I could only get my husband to understand that simple concept."

"I think it's all very exciting," Lucy said.

"Which is why Ma and Pa keep you at home." The last thing the town needed was Lucy running around unsupervised. Ward had a feeling his little sister could come close to Katie in the adventure department.

Chapter 14

The sound of bedclothes rustling woke Katie. She groaned and pulled the blankets over her head. After staying up too late going over every detail of her afternoon with the Alston family, she wanted to sleep. But work called, and she wasn't one to shirk her duties.

Fifteen minutes later, she was dressed and headed to the kitchen to grab her own breakfast before readying the dining room for guests. With the arrival of fall, she woke to a morning still dark and a chill in the air.

In the kitchen, she grabbed two biscuits, spread them with fresh apple butter and stepped outside to breathe in the fresh air before the rush of the day. She glanced in the direction of the Alston farm. Although it was over a thirty-minute ride by car, she could picture the lovely place in her mind. Yesterday had been one of the best days of her life, despite Ward's aggravation at knowing what had beset her in the woods. He'd barely spoken two words when bringing her back to town.

Still, knowing he cared about her welfare warmed her. She smiled and brushed the crumbs from her hand. Maybe, once the whole thing with Amos was taken care of, there was the chance of a relationship with Ward after all.

Finished, she headed back inside. Miss Alston grinned at her from where she supervised a new girl rolling silverware. "How was your time with my family? They seem to adore you, and I heard you rode alone in Ward's automobile."

"It was lovely, thank you. Your parents are very kind." Katie's face heated. Must she blush every time there was the slightest mention of Ward? What a silly ninny she was. "The Ford is rather frightening."

Miss Alston nodded. "But exciting, despite the smell of the fuel it uses." She bit her lip. "I hope you don't think I'm overstepping my boundaries, but Ward told me of the predicament you're in." She held up a hand when Katie opened her mouth to protest. "I don't think badly of you, at all. Don't worry. My brother will get to the bottom of it."

"My stepfather is a very convincing man." So, Ward had told his sister to keep an eye on her. How dare he bring others into her troubles? Her breakfast sat like a rock in her stomach.

Despite her resolve not to let thoughts of Ward ruin a good day, she couldn't help but go through the motions of working. Every time the train whistle blew, announcing a new crowd of diners, she cringed. Seeing Amos on his usual stool at the counter didn't help. She still wanted to dump a pitcher of water over his head. She knew for a fact he was the one who had hired the three men to scare her in the woods. Who else would want to frighten her?

It wouldn't do any good. He might have taken away one of the joys from her daily schedule, but she refused to allow the man to make her cower. Instead, she was almost tempted to hand over the deed to her land just to get him to leave town. Eventually, one of them would have to leave, and she didn't want it to be her. She'd already fallen in love with Somerville.

She put a hand over her hidden pocket, thankful the deed was the one slip of paper she hadn't pulled from her pocket at the creek. It still crinkled reassuringly next to her leg.

Ward walked in, for his morning coffee, no doubt. Katie turned her back and pretended to be busy straightening clean glasses. She'd need to compose herself before facing him.

Miss Alston met her gaze. "I'm sorry," she mouthed.

Katie shrugged. It wasn't the head waitress's fault. Ward should know when to keep his mouth shut. He as a Texas Ranger, after all. She stormed into the kitchen.

The chef glanced up, took one look at her face and turned back to chopping vegetables with earnest. Good. Katie was in no mood for conversation. She slipped into her normal hiding place when she wanted a breather and closed the pantry door.

Closing her eyes, she prayed for peace and a rein on her temper. Tears pricked her eyes. She felt cheated somehow. An emotion that made no sense, since Ward was only doing his job.

Was Miss Alston only kind to her in hopes that Katie would confide in her? Give her information she could repeat to her brother? Did no one care for Katie for herself?

One of the sermons from a past Sunday flickered through her brain, the sermon that spoke of turning one's burdens over to God. Maybe Katie kept too tight a rein on things. God's shoulders were stronger than hers. She prayed for Him to take the reins of the situation involving Amos. She didn't want to be in control anymore. She might have to make it a daily decision to turn things over, but it was bound to be easier.

Feeling more able to do her job, she headed back to the dining room as the dinner crowd swarmed into the restaurant. Two hours more and she could hide in the common room and work on her dress. The rhythmic motions of the sewing machine never failed to calm her.

The customers at her two tables that evening were demanding, wanting this and that, never completely satisfied with anything Katie put in front of them. Nevertheless, she kept her smile pasted on and scurried back and forth from the kitchen. By the time the last customer left, exhaustion weighed her shoulders and her feet hurt.

She untied her apron and tossed it with the others to be laundered. She pushed through the door and came face-to-face with Ward. "May I help you?" She hoped he'd know by the coolness of her tone she didn't want to speak with him.

"I'm here to take you on your nightly walk."

Katie's mouth opened and then closed. Her eyes hardened. "Good. We need to talk." She stormed past him and out the door. Outside, she turned and planted her fists on her slim hips. "Where?"

"The creek?" Surely she wouldn't be frightened to go into the woods with him.

She marched ahead of him, shoulders straight, head held high. What had he done to warrant her anger?

"I don't want to sit," she said when they'd arrived beside the creek. "You want to walk so we'll walk."

He stopped her with a hand on her arm. "What is wrong? Have I done something?"

"Why did you tell your sister about the charges against me?"

He should have known Caroline wouldn't keep her mouth shut. "That was the day you arrived."

"Her kindness to me is only a ploy, same as yours."

Katie picked up a rock and tossed it into the creek. A piece of paper fluttered by, the word *Wanted* barely legible. Katie gasped.

Ward retrieved the sheet before it drifted out of sight. "I wonder how this got here. It's against the law to remove wanted posters from where they're posted." Katie jerked, her face ghostly under the moon's light. "Katie?" He could barely make out the outline of a woman.

"I took it. I also took one of a man I believe to be Amos, although it was from a long time ago and bears a different name." She lifted her chin, tears shimmering in her eyes. "Are you going to arrest me?"

He didn't know what to do. He felt certain she hadn't known she was breaking the law. But why take the poster if she were innocent? Add in that ignorance was no excuse for criminal behavior, and he found himself at odds. His job said he needed to arrest her, his heart said to let things be. With a sigh, he tore the soggy paper into pieces and tossed them back into the creek.

Katie relaxed and swiped a hand across her eyes. "It said I was wanted for questioning, so question me."

He shook his head. The Harvey Company only hired girls with good moral character. If Katie was a wanted woman, how had they overlooked it? He ran his fingers through his hair. Things didn't make sense. His boss was right. Ward couldn't let go of his emotions in the case to see things clearly. "Did you steal from Amos Moore?"

"The land is mine. I gave back the money, although he claims he never received it." She plopped on a fallen log, her dark dress billowing around her. "He says my mother deeded the land to him, but I know that to be a lie. I haven't seen a single thing to support his claims. We've gone over this."

He sat next to her, and she scooted as far away as the

log would allow. His heart sank. "I need to know everything if I'm going to help you."

"You'll help me?" She cut him a sideways glance. "As a friend, or as a Ranger?"

"Can't I do both? I'd like to see justice served."

She leaped to her feet. "Then see Amos put behind bars."

He stood and met her furious gaze. "I don't have enough evidence."

"Ha. Have you even brought the man in for questioning?"

"Some. He says you're the crook. It's his word against yours." How had he gotten himself into this mess? Oh, yeah. He was a fool for a pretty face and big dark eyes.

"Of course he does." She set off down the path at a quick pace, her arms wrapped around herself.

He jogged to catch up, removing his jacket. "Are you cold?"

"I don't want your coat."

He grabbed her arm and swung her around. "I said I was sorry."

She studied his face. "Okay."

That was it? She was letting him off the hook?

A twig snapped. He jerked and thrust Katie behind him. "Shh."

The three rough men he'd noticed getting off the train a few days ago emerged from the brush. The largest one laughed. "Look, boys, she brought a friend this time."

Ward pulled his badge from his pocket and flashed it at them. "I suggest you boys move on."

"It's three against one. I think we can take you." The man pulled a revolver from his waistband. "We came prepared this time."

Ward felt Katie fumbling behind him. Soon she stood next to him, a pistol in her hand. "Give that to me." The woman was crazy. Her breath came in gasps and her hand trembled as she handed over the weapon. How had she managed to pull the trigger before? "What do you three want?"

"The girl."

"Can't have her." Ward aimed the gun. "Tell that to whoever sent you. They want her, they can go through me."

The other two men pulled their guns.

Ward could take down one, maybe two, but the third would win. He backed up slowly, ushering Katie along with him. These three were brazen and had most likely been watching the trail for days. He'd thought for sure they wouldn't bother if he was along. He was wrong, and he sure didn't relish getting shot again.

"When I say jump, jump into the water," he whispered.

"It's freezing," Katie said.

"Better than a bullet, wouldn't you say?" He knew of an overhang in deeper water just a few yards away. "Are you men up to murder? Because if you don't kill me, I'll hunt you down like the scum you are."

One of the men faltered. "I ain't here to kill anyone." He backed away. Soon one of the other two followed.

The third man shook his head and cursed. "We ain't getting paid. I ain't messing with a Ranger."

They turned and crashed through the brush.

The night was too dark for Ward to have seen their faces. Against his better judgment, he handed Katie back her gun. "Things sure aren't boring around you, Katie Gamble. Life with you suits your name. It's a gamble for sure."

Chapter 15

"What a long week." Katie slipped under the covers of her bed. Every muscle in her body ached. "Thank goodness it's Saturday night."

"I'm sleeping forever tomorrow." Sarah pulled her blankets to her chin. "I never knew so many people traveled by train until working in a Harvey restaurant."

Katie hadn't either. She wiggled her chilled toes and waited for the thick quilts to warm her. While the rooms in the dormitory were comfortable, they weren't heated as well as she'd like. She glanced at the clock on her nightstand and groaned. Ten o'clock. Morning would come too early. Again.

She'd just finished the last adjustments on her new dress. The yellow of the fabric barely cut through the gloom of the room. She smiled, envisioning Ward's eyes when he saw her in it at church. She shivered. Her next purchase would be a thick coat.

Sleep finally came, along with dreams of Ward. In her

dreams, he fully believed her innocence and put Amos behind bars. Then, he held out his hand and declared—

Her eyes flew open. Was that smoke? She flung aside the blankets and sniffed. Thin tendrils of grey smoke drifted under the door. Shouts of "Fire!" rang through the halls.

She leaped from the bed. "Sarah!"

"What?"

"Fire! Get up." Katie slipped her feet into her slippers and flung the slip with her hidden pocket over her shoulder. Grabbing her new dress, she turned. "Let's go."

Sarah's eyes were wide as she scrambled to collect what she could. "What should I take?"

"Yourself. If you don't have it now, it's too late." Katie yanked open the door.

People raced past, some burdened with belongings, others with nothing but the nightclothes on their back. Miss Alston stopped at their door. "Come on, girls. It's spreading fast." She ushered them ahead of her.

Katie's heart lodged in her throat as she passed a wall fully engulfed in flames. She hugged the opposite wall and headed down the stairs as fast as she could, Sarah and the head waitress on her heels. Were they the last to leave the building? Had she and Sarah slept that soundly?

Bells clanged as the fire department rushed in their direction, the new red truck skidding to a stop. Ward waited outside and pulled Katie and his sister to safety. Katie glanced over her shoulder. "Sarah."

"I'm here." The petite blonde collapsed in a heap on the sidewalk opposite the dormitory.

By now, the roof was burning, and flames licked the sky. Katie shuddered, hugging her slip and dress. She was no longer cold. The heat from the inferno warmed her, even across the street. She watched as water was pumped onto the dormitory and surrounding buildings in an attempt to save what could be saved.

Miss Alston circulated among the Harvey employees, along with the manager, making sure everyone was accounted for. When she'd finished, she leaned against the building beside Katie. "This is horrible."

"Where will we stay?" Sarah hugged her knees. "Our uniforms are gone, our personal belongings, everything."

"Don't worry." Katie put an arm around her shoulders. "We'll manage. The good thing is that everyone made it out unharmed." All her money, shoved in a metal box under the bed, was burned to a crisp. Unless God had mercy and had spared the box. At least she had the deed. She felt the slip for the reassuring crinkle.

Ward ran by, a bucket in each hand. He spared them a glance but didn't stop.

"We should help." Katie got to her feet. "We can fill buckets or wet blankets."

"I can't." Sarah cried, tears leaving tracks in the soot on her face.

"Then sit here and watch my things." Katie glanced at Miss Alston, who nodded.

"That's a great idea, Katie." Together they hurried to the well.

Their arrival freed a couple of men to leave to fight the fire. Soon, Katie had a rhythm of fill a bucket, soak a blanket, fill a bucket, and on and on until she thought her arms would fall off.

"You ladies are incredible." Ward returned for what seemed like his hundredth bucket. Katie had long ago lost track. "But you should rest."

"Are you going to rest?" She handed another man a soaked blanket.

"Not until the fire is out."

"Then neither will I." She glanced to where Sarah had

Katie's dress draped around her shoulders. She prayed the other girl wouldn't remove the gun or deed from the pocket of the slip. She knew she was taking a chance leaving them, but the firefighters needed help. She ducked her head and continued working.

"You're doing a wonderful job, Katie." Ward placed a hand on her shoulder, then dashed back to the fire, which thankfully had been contained to only the dormitory.

"I'm sure the hotel will give the girls a place to stay." Miss Alston planted her hands on her hips and leaned back. "As for uniforms, hopefully every girl had at least one at the laundress."

Katie nodded, enjoying the other woman's company, but still hesitant to say anything for fear of it getting back to Ward, no matter how trivial. The fact the two had been sharing information since her arrival still rankled.

A mighty groan sounded behind her. She whirled in time to see the roof collapse. So that was it. Nothing left but smoldering boards to douse. She filled a few more buckets and plopped down next to Sarah.

The other girl handed her back her things. "Why do you have a gun?"

Katie shrugged. "A single girl can't be too careful, can she?"

"I suppose not." She glanced around the milling crowd. "I haven't seen Rachel. I hope she's all right."

"Miss Alston said everyone was accounted for." Katie had never been so tired in her life. She bent her knees and rested her cheek on top of them.

"Katie." Ward shook her awake. "It's time to take you to the hotel."

She nodded and stood, then collapsed.

Ward caught her as she fell. Exhausted, poor thing. He cradled her against his chest and motioned for Sarah to follow. Soon, he laid Katie on a bed provided for her and Sarah to share in a spare room of the hotel. He turned and met his sister's gaze. "She's a trouper, this one."

"She is." Caroline sighed. "I'm tired myself. The restaurant will have to run on a skeleton crew tomorrow. I don't have the energy to hunt up uniforms."

"They can wait." He escorted her to another vacant room. "Get some rest. I'll see you in the morning."

With the women settled, Ward marched outside, ignoring his own exhaustion, and walked the perimeter of the burned section of the building. Witnesses said the fire spread quickly. Ward searched the surrounding area, widening his search with every circle.

There it was. Hidden under a thick bush was a gas can. Just as he'd suspected, the fire had been started on purpose. Thankfully, no one had been injured, and the only part uninhabitable was the women's dormitory. He clenched his fists and went in search of the sheriff.

He found the man speaking with a few of the firefighters who had yet to head home. They all stared as Ward strode into their midst. "The fire was started deliberately. I found this gas can behind the building."

"That's what we suspected," the fire chief said. "But why would anyone want to burn down the Harvey Girls' dormitory?"

Ward suspected it all had to do with Katie, but he held his tongue in case he was wrong. It wouldn't do to have her brought in for questioning until he was more certain of the motive.

He'd heard rumors of a nefarious woman in yellow who took men's poker money and swindled shop keepers, having gotten them to trust her with her sweet smile. Not only had his heart almost stopped when he'd spotted Katie and his sister fleeing the fire, but also when he'd spotted Katie carrying a yellow dress. He rubbed both hands over his face, trying to clear the confusion from his mind. Of course the mysterious woman wasn't Katie. Just about everyone in town knew the beautiful Harvey waitresses.

His heart told him one thing, his mind another. Until he knew for sure, he couldn't shove aside the possibility that the charges against Katie were true. He needed to spend time in prayer, but time slowed for no man, and Ward's gut told him that things were drawing to an explosive conclusion. Soon.

"We'll investigate," the fire chief said. "And let you both know what we find. For now, we'd best all get to our beds."

Unable to sleep, Ward had raced over on horseback the moment he'd spotted smoke from his bedroom window. By the time he'd arrived in town, both he and the horse were whipped. He had no desire to ride back home. He put the horse into the sleepy hands of the livery owner, and booked a hotel room of his own. "You're lucky, mister," the elderly man behind the counter said. "Because of the fire, we're almost filled up." He handed Ward a key. "Those Harvey Company employees filled an entire floor. But the money is good, so I'm not complaining."

"Thank you." Ward headed down a hall and unlocked a room half the size of his bedroom at home. But the bed looked clean and the washbasin was full. He set the key on bureau and washed the soot from his face and arms. There was no help for his clothes until he made it back to the farm.

He toed off his boots and then shed his clothes, not wanting to dirty the bed with soot. He crossed his arms under his head and stared at the ceiling, picturing Katie's face. She'd done the work of a man filling buckets. That didn't fit in with his idea of a criminal. But, he supposed, even criminals worked hard if it suited their purpose.

Katie needed to let Ward have a look at the deed. If he

could compare it to the one Amos claimed to have, maybe he could determine which one was a forgery.

Was there really a wanted poster with Amos's face but with a different name? Since Katie had taken it upon herself to rip the poster from the wall, Ward would have to travel to a different town to see for himself.

Did he have enough time? He rolled over and punched his pillow. Why couldn't Katie have been simple? A woman he could fall for and even contemplate settling down with? He could finally admit to himself that he cared for her too much for a man in charge of checking out her story. It was becoming harder and harder to be unbiased.

He sighed and dreaded the long hours until dawn. He'd get little sleep if his mind didn't stop whirring like the tires on his Ford. He smiled, remembering Katie's nervousness when he'd taken her for a ride.

Had the men in the woods meant to harm her, or were they there to meet her? With banks being robbed up and down the railroad, Ward had heard tales of a woman robber. One with dark hair, carrying a handgun. Add to those the rumors of a woman in a yellow dress coercing the men of Somerville from their money, and it didn't look good for Katie if Amos convinced the townsfolk that Katie was the woman in yellow.

Not at all.

Chapter 16

"Since we're having such an unusually warm day for November, we're having a picnic." Lucy bounced up to Katie after church. "We're inviting you to come along." The freckles across her nose were highlighted by the afternoon sun, adding a delightful impish look to the young girl's face. "Please say you'll come."

Katie glanced to where Ward stood with his family. All common sense told her to say no, but it was a beautiful day, and loneliness tended to plague her on such days. "I'd be delighted." She ran her hands down her yellow dress, and deemed it fitting, even with the small burned hole at the hem. Of course, the only other thing she had to wear was a plain housedress that had been donated by the ladies auxiliary, which wouldn't do.

"Come on." Lucy grabbed her hand. "We're headed to the lake right now."

Katie allowed herself to be dragged along. To her relief, Ward's automobile was nowhere in sight. Instead, he helped her into the back of the wagon and climbed in beside her. She didn't know which was worse—being bounced in the car until her teeth rattled or having her shoulder pressed against Ward's.

The musky scent of his aftershave sent her senses soaring. The early November day seemed brighter, colors more vibrant and the chatter of folks milling in the churchyard more festive. She took a deep breath. Despite the cloud hanging over her head regarding Amos's accusations, and his suspicious absence since the fire, she would enjoy the day if it killed her.

The Somerville lake sparkled under the sun as if someone had cast diamonds across the surface. A slight breeze rippled the water and whispered through the tree branches. Why hadn't Katie made time to visit the lake before? The serenity of the place soothed her nerves, despite the way her hand felt in Ward's as he helped her from the wagon.

When Mrs. Alston refused her help in setting up the picnic, Katie moved to the water's edge. A fish flopped to her right and a hawk dove to the water's surface, its claws skimming as it grasped its wiggling prey.

"It's beautiful," she whispered.

"Yes, she is." Ward smiled down at her.

Her face heated, and she turned her attention back to the water. "We have ponds back home, but nothing like this."

"I'd like to take you for a boat ride after lunch, if you're willing."

She tilted her head. If she was nothing more than a job to him, why did he act as if they were courting? Lovers took boat rides, not a Texas Ranger and his suspect. Her tongue betrayed her. "I'd like that." If they spent enough time together, maybe he would see she was innocent of Amos's ridiculous charges. The hard part would be keeping her heart from racing when Ward gazed at her with his soft hazel eyes.

"Are you hungry? Ma made fried chicken."

"Starving."

Ward placed his hand on the small of her back and guided her to a worn quilt spread on the dry grass. For a few hours, Katie would pretend they were nothing more than a man and woman getting to know each other.

Mrs. Alston handed her a chicken leg along with a roll and a healthy dollop of potato salad kept cool in a crock set inside a pail of water. Katie's stomach rumbled at the sight of the home prepared food. The restaurant served well-made meals, but sometimes a simple meal under the sun was the best.

The family's chatter about life on their farm put Katie at ease. She met Mrs. Alston's smile and returned it with one of her own. What Katie wouldn't give to sit across from her own mother and converse about the goals for the week or the highlights of the past days. She stared back at the lake. She'd forfeit the deed to the land to have her mother back.

"You look sad, Katie." Mrs. Alston placed a hand over hers. "Are you feeling all right?"

"I'm fine, thank you. Missing my own mother." She took a deep breath and dropped her chicken bone into a nearby pail. "She died of consumption back in the spring. Pa the year before."

"You poor thing." She gave Katie's hand a pat. "We'll be your family. A woman can never have enough daughters."

"I could use another man in the family." Ward laughed. "Pa and I are outnumbered."

While Mrs. Alston's words were meant to comfort, they only served to remind Katie that she was there under the supervision of Ward. But the lure of a surrogate family was strong.

"Okay, folks." Ward stood and brushed crumbs off his tan pants. "I promised Katie a boat ride. We'll be back in a bit to help load everything back into the wagon." He held down a hand to pull her to her feet. "Ready?"

"Yes." She allowed him to keep hold of her hand as he led her to a small boat tied to a bush. "It doesn't look very sturdy. I'm not a strong swimmer." Especially not in a dress.

"You'll be safe with me." He helped her into the boat.

It rocked under her feet, and she crawled the last bit until she reached her seat. Very becoming, she was sure. Thankfully, Ward's attention was on untying the rope.

Once they were free, he used one of the paddles to push them away from the shore where his strong strokes sent them into deeper water. Katie gripped the sides of the boat until her knuckles hurt. As Ward's smooth paddling propelled them with little rocking, she slowly released her hold and prepared to enjoy the ride.

Once they were out in the middle of the lake, Ward laid the paddles across his knees. "Are you feeling okay? No motion sickness?"

"None at all, thank you."

Ward didn't like deceiving Katie and tricking her into a boat ride so he could get her alone and in a place she couldn't run away, but he didn't have a choice. They needed to get to the bottom of Amos's accusations. The man's suspicious absence since the fire looked favorable for Katie, but Ward wanted to dispel any lingering doubts about her innocence.

"Do you have the deed with you?"

"Yes." She narrowed her eyes.

"May I see it?"

"It isn't easily accessible." She crossed her arms.

If glares could kill, he'd have a knife in his gut for sure. "I'll close my eyes while you fish it out of your hidden pocket."

"How did you—? Oh, never mind. Don't look."

He closed his eyes and turned away. The sound of rustling clothes mingled with the shriek of a hawk.

"Here."

He opened his eyes and took the wrinkled paper from her hand. "It's signed with an *X*."

"Pa couldn't read or write, but he told me the land was mine." Tears shimmered in her eyes. "Ma would have never given it to Amos."

"This doesn't look good, Katie." He handed it back to her. "Without a legitimate signature, I'm not sure a judge would look seriously at it. If Amos has another deed with your mother's signature—"

"He can't have it!" She leaped to her feet, sending the boat rocking wildly from side to side.

Ward grabbed her arm. "Sit down before you tip us."

He didn't know what to think. Katie's deed probably looked more forged than Amos's or he'd eat his hat. It wasn't hard to put an *X* on a document. He studied her face.

She gazed at the water, spots of color high on her cheeks. Her display of temper told him that anger simmered under the surface of that beautiful face. Who was this woman? Was she really just a mountain girl out to save what was hers or out to take what she believed to be hers? Was she a thief? A bank robber out to steal from hard-working folks, or was she only concerned about holding on to her family land? Katie Gamble was a mystery, and Ward was as lost as ever.

She faced him. "Are you going to help me, or arrest me? This back-and-forth game you're playing is driving me insane."

"I want to help you, I really do, but—"

Tears escaped, and he wanted nothing more than to brush them away from her smooth cheek. "So, I've nothing to prove I'm right."

"It'll be hard."

"I'm not afraid of hard." She folded her hands in her lap. "I won't give up."

He glanced toward the shoreline, where a woman in a bright yellow dress conversed with a man. He couldn't make out the woman's features, but she looked a lot like Katie from a distance.

"That looks like Rachel, one of the other waitresses," she said.

"How many girls in town have yellow dresses?"

She looked taken aback at the question. "I'm sure I don't know. It's a popular color. Are you now questioning the colors women choose to wear?"

"No." He straightened. "There's a woman wearing a yellow dress and robbing men at poker games while they're drunk."

"Drunk men at poker games don't deserve to hold on to their money."

That statement did not help her case any. The wind began to pick up as clouds built on the horizon. "We'd best head back. Weather's changing."

"Good. I've had enough of this afternoon, thank you very much." She tilted her pretty chin and didn't look at him again. Not even when they reached the shore and he helped her from the boat.

She stepped around him and marched back to the rest of the family. From the look on his ma's face, he'd have some questions to answer later. How much should he tell her? How would she react when he told her Katie was at the center of his investigation? She'd probably side with Caroline.

Sometimes, women couldn't see the logical side of things. The women in his family probably only saw a pleasant girl without a family.

On the ride home, Caroline sat in the back with him

and let Katie sit with Ma and Pa. "What happened on the lake? Katie looked darker than a thundercloud, and don't think Ma didn't notice. She did."

"I asked her to show me the deed." He kept his voice low. "It's only signed with an *X.* How can any judge make a determination based on that? Especially if there is a signed deed floating around somewhere. She also said some other things that made her look guilty. I'm as confused as ever."

"You need to take your heart out of the situation."

"Explain." Ward scooted until he could see her face.

"You care for Katie." She shook her head. "Don't give me that look. You know you do, and the fact that you care muddles things for you. You're used to the lines of good and bad being clearly drawn. In this case they're as crooked as the part in Lucy's hair."

"How did you get to be so wise?"

"I'm the oldest. It comes with the territory." She leaned closer. "Ma just thinks y'all had a lover's spat. Best to leave it at that and say you'll apologize at the earliest convenience. You do not want to tell her Katie is a suspect."

Ward nodded. That wouldn't go over well at all. He glanced at the wagon seat and Katie's ramrod spine. Caroline was right. He did care, and it was messing everything up.

Chapter 17

What was she doing in Somerville? Her plan to travel to some faraway town had led to nothing but heartache. Amos continued to plague her and now Ward doubted she was innocent. Though she'd heard rumors that the sheriff and judge back home were crooked, Katie should have taken her chances and asked for help. She set a plate of biscuits and gravy in front of a man with his nose buried in the paper. She might as well request a transfer, start somewhere new, and forget all about the land. What could a single girl do with two hundred acres anyway, oil rights or not? But no, she'd worked too hard to give up now, especially to a snake like Amos.

The man folded the paper, and Katie caught a glimpse of the front page. Another bank robbery yesterday. She stared out the front window of the restaurant. In her heart she suspected Amos was smack-dab in the middle of the robberies, not as Amos Moore, but as Burt Kilroy.

Ward entered the dining room and nodded in her direction before taking a seat at the counter. Good. He was almost the last person she wanted to talk to that morning, especially after his doubting questions the day before. She motioned for the drink girl to refill her customer's coffee, and then headed outside.

The warmth of the day before had fled just as her sense of peace in the town had. She had two months left on her contract. Could she transfer before then, or should she wait it out, leaving the Harvey Company for good when the contract expired? She could head somewhere remote, like Montana, and begin a new life. She was resourceful. She could make a living for herself.

Maybe she'd turn around and head home. Surely somebody would pay her for the oil under the surface of her land. That should be enough to set her up for life. All she needed to do was get Amos to leave her alone. But how would she do that? He was as determined as she was.

She rubbed her eyes as if she could erase the confusion. When she opened her eyes again, she focused on the church steeple at the end of the road. After informing Miss Alston she needed a break and would return in a while, she hung her apron on a hook in the kitchen and marched toward the church. A conversation with God was long overdue.

The sanctuary was empty on a Monday morning. Katie took a seat in the first pew and picked up the Bible lying there. She flipped through the pages, not sure exactly what she was looking for. The pages fell open to the psalms and her gaze fell on Hebrews 13:6. So we can say for sure, "The Lord is my Helper, I am not afraid of anything man can do to me."

She raised her head and gazed at the simple cross hanging behind the podium. For the first time since fleeing her home, Katie felt the peace she'd sought. She could hear her mother whispering in her ear that she should have sought

God a long time ago. That His Word held all the answers she could ever need.

But fear carried a lot of weight. Katie vowed to never have that kind of fear again. From that moment forward she would trust God to guide her steps. He was much more capable than she was. She closed the Bible and stood. "Thank you," she said to the cross. "I should never have doubted."

She stepped into the late-morning sun and shaded her eyes. A man ran through the trees beside the church, a bandana around his nose and mouth. Before Katie could blink, another followed the first. She withdrew back into the church.

Why would two masked men be running around the perimeter of the town?

The bank.

She needed to raise the alarm without them seeing her. But how? She lifted her dress and withdrew the Mauser. What was she doing? She leaned against the pew. She couldn't dash out there like a fool brandishing a pistol. This wasn't the 1800s.

Shots rang out, and she gripped the gun tighter. Would they come inside the church and find her? She peered out the window. Two more men had joined the others and they barged through the bank doors. Screams reached Katie's ears.

Another shot. She had to do something. Taking a deep breath, she raced from the church and around to the back of the bank. If she snuck in the back door... No, she needed to get Ward. She switched directions, entering the street from a narrow alley. "The bank is being robbed!"

Several heads turned in her direction. She shouted a warning again and shot from the alley like a bullet.

She bumped into a woman taking refuge under an awning. The woman shrieked, and fainted. Now what was Katie supposed to do? If she stayed to help, the robbers would get away, if she left, the woman would think her uncaring.

She patted the woman's cheek as more shots rang out. "Please, wake up." When the woman's eyelids fluttered, Katie resumed her mad dash across the street. Dodging horses and buggies, she burst into the restaurant.

Bending over to catch her breath, she searched the room for Ward. "The...bank. Where's...Ward?"

Miss Alston helped her to a chair. "He ran out with the first gunshots. Put your gun away, dear, you're frightening the customers."

Katie met the head waitress's cold gaze. All the customers were crowded around the window. She stashed her pistol. Miss Alston believed her a part of the robbery. What else could she think when she stormed into the restaurant with a gun in her hand?

"Don't move, Katie." Miss Alston laid a heavy hand on her shoulder. "Ward will be back soon."

"Miss Alston, I wasn't—"

She shook her head. "Talk to Ward."

Katie's eyes burned. All she'd wanted to do was help. Now she found herself in more trouble than before. Did Miss Alston expect her to sit at a dining table until Ward returned?

She glanced at the crowd gathered by the window. What would they think when they returned to their seats? "I'll be in the kitchen." She rushed from the room and out the back door to sit on the steps. The day was cool, but it was a better place to wait for condemnation than in full view of everyone.

Ward had dashed outside at the sound of the first shot and made a beeline for the bank. He shoved his way through spectators clogging the streets. Didn't these people know to take cover when there was gunfire?

By the time he reached the bank, the robbers had left, taking with them several thousands of dollars. He checked to make sure no one was injured then raced back outside.

Katie sprinted across the street with a gun in her hand and disappeared through the doors of the restaurant. His heart sank. Clearly, she had been at the bank. How could he have been so stupid as to believe her lies?

"We'll need you to help us round up this gang," the sheriff called after him. "That fella you've been looking for? One of the bank tellers said he's one of the robbers. Looks like the man's a crook after all. Where are you going? We need your help."

Ward held up a hand to signify he'd heard. He planned on doing everything in his power to catch the crooks, but first he had something else to do.

Steps heavy, he headed back to the restaurant. A woman stopped him and told him of how she was accosted by one of the Harvey Girls with a gun. Ward sighed and continued on his way. Caroline met him the moment he walked in.

"She's out back, unless she's run off." Sadness caused lines in her face.

"You aren't watching her?" Ward frowned and glanced toward the kitchen.

"I have a job to do out here. I told her to stay put, but she left anyway." She crossed her arms and glared. "Do you want me to say you were right and I was wrong?"

He shook his head. "This pains me more than you can imagine." He pushed through the kitchen door and found Katie exactly where Caroline had said she would be.

Tear tracks lined her pretty face. Ward refused to be swayed by her emotions or her beauty. "I guess you heard the bank was robbed."

"I didn't hear it, I saw it." She refused to look at him. "I had nothing to do with robbing the bank."

"Where were you?"

"At the church praying about my situation, but I don't expect you to believe me." She stood and dusted off the back of her dress.

"I suppose there was nobody around that could testify to that fact?" At the shake of her head, he continued. "I have an eye witness who said one of the Harvey Girls accosted her at gunpoint."

"That was an accident. I was running—"

"To escape the scene?"

"No, to find you." She planted her fists on her hips and met his glare. "At first I intended to try to stop the robbery, but realized that was stupid, so I ran back to the street and knocked the woman over."

He shook his head. A single woman trying to stop several armed men? Not likely. Miss Gamble belonged on the stage, so convincing were her story and facial expressions. "That sounds ludicrous."

"I was at the church praying. When I was getting ready to leave, I spotted several men in the woods. I pulled my gun—"

"And joined them?"

"Stop interrupting me. No, I didn't join them. Why would I? I'm not a crook, Ward." She huffed and turned her back to him.

"You were seen fleeing the crime scene, you attacked a woman and then you burst into the restaurant with your gun drawn. I have enough witnesses that it would take me hours to interview them all. None of this makes you appear innocent."

"What about the witnesses in the bank? Maybe you should ask them if I was there." She whirled to face him.

"It's quite possible you acted as nothing more than a lookout." He steeled himself not to respond to the tears spilling down her cheeks or the dejected slant of her shoulders. He'd been enough of a fool to be taken in by her charms.

"Now what?"

"I don't know." He'd never arrested a woman before. He caught a glimpse of Caroline watching through the back door and waved her outside.

Without looking at Katie, she said, "Several of the customers at the window said they spotted a dark-haired woman fleeing the bank. A woman in black."

Katie sniffed. "I'm not the only dark-haired woman in town."

"But you are wearing black and own a yellow dress. All of which fit the woman committing crimes in this town." Ward was torn. Should he arrest her, or demand she stay in her room until the marshal arrived?

"That's all circumstantial evidence. While you're wasting time with me, the real culprits are getting away. You should be focusing your attentions on finding Amos Moore, aka Burt Kilroy."

Ward knew that name. "Is that the wanted poster you tore off the wall in the mercantile? Other than yours, of course."

"Yes, I told you that. You can ask me a million times and my story will not change." She glanced at Caroline, who turned away.

"Your services are no longer needed within the Harvey Company, Miss Gamble. Please pack your belongings at your earliest convenience." Caroline stormed back into the restaurant.

Katie slumped onto the steps and covered her face.

Ward watched, unclear as to how to proceed. If she were a man, he'd take her to jail for questioning. As it was, he didn't know if the Somerville jail had ever held a woman. How would the townspeople react if he marched Katie across the street? Would they merely stare, or throw stones?

Before he could make up his mind what to do, she bolted.

It took a second before it registered in his mind that she meant to flee. He sprinted after her, catching her around the waist and taking them both to the ground.

She kicked and shrieked like a bobcat. "Let go of me."

Her legs flailed against his shins, her elbows against his ribs. One connected with the almost healed wound in his side. He hissed against the sharp pain. "Stop fighting. You're only making it worse."

"I don't care." She pounded at his arms around her.

"Why did you attempt to run?" She had to know he would catch her. Keeping a tight grip on her arm, he got up and yanked her to her feet. "Hand me your gun or I'll go after it."

"You wouldn't dare."

He narrowed his eyes. "Try me." Couldn't she see what this was doing to him? How his heart lay in shattered pieces at her feet?

"Turn around." She tilted her chin.

"I will not."

She gasped then lifted her dress and pulled her pistol from the pocket of her slip. She handed it to him handle first. "See? I could just as easily have shot you. I don't know why I ran. I'm frightened, I suppose."

"Miss Katie Gamble, you're under arrest."

Chapter 18

Katie lay on the hard cot and rolled into a ball. She didn't know why she'd tried to run. Fear had consumed her and her only thought had been to get away. Now her tears soaked the thin mattress while night fell outside the barred window.

She had nothing now. Ward, the fiend, had confiscated her gun and the deed. Most likely he'd turn the precious sheet of paper over to Amos, if he could find the crook. She brushed her hand angrily across her face.

Refusing to wallow in self-pity for a moment longer, she sat up and scooted against the wall, hugging her knees. God had promised that no man could harm her. No, that wasn't right. The last scripture she'd read said she shouldn't *be afraid* of what men could do to her. But she was. She was very afraid.

"Psst."

Katie dashed to the window. Sarah grinned up at her.

"Is it true you were part of the robbery?" Her pretty smile didn't fade.

"Of course not." Katie gripped the bars.

"That's what I told everyone, but some of the fools wouldn't listen. Now, it seems that man who's been harassing you has skipped town. Here, I brought you some food." She handed a sandwich through the bars. "I tried to come through the front door, but they—" She glanced to her left and dashed away as Ward marched around the corner.

Katie stuffed the sandwich down her bodice, and glared. Why was he still here? Shouldn't he be off to parts unknown now that he had his "crook" behind bars?

"Who was that?" Ward stared in the direction Sarah had fled.

"A gawker. Don't worry. They didn't give me anything to use to dig myself out." She wanted to rattle the bars and demand he release her.

Ward rubbed his hands over his face. "I'm only doing my job, Katie. I wish you understood that."

"Well, you aren't very good at it." She gripped the bars so tight her knuckles ached. Tears stung her eyes. She blinked them back, refusing to cry in front of the man who had arrested her. The man she thought she loved, and who she thought maybe was starting to return those feelings.

"It's for your own good."

She snorted, and withdrew back to her cot. The sandwich was very welcome, and she devoured it quickly before Ward found out and took it from her.

How had her life come to this? Katie Gamble, in a jail cell, eating smuggled-in food? Despite her resolve to stay strong, the tears fell anew. Ma must have been tossing in her grave, and Amos laughing his fool head off.

Not caring about the crumbs in her lap, Katie stretched out on the cot. Time passed slowly, and she counted the wood slats above her. Thirty-three.

The sun set and cast the room into darkness. A tiny

sliver of light came from the sheriff's office, providing a little relief from the dark. Sleep evaded her. Instead her mind whirled, trying to find a way out of her current predicament. Oh, why had she run?

Maybe tears would have worked better. Outrage at Ward's questions had only fueled the fire of his belief that she was guilty. She should have stayed in the church instead of trying to warn people. A Harvey Girl uniform was too conspicuous for her to have been running around town brandishing her weapon. How stupid could one girl be?

She tried to keep her fear at bay, but as the night lengthened, it became harder and harder. When the sheriff turned off the one light in the building, casting Katie into dark so deep she couldn't see her hand in front of her face, she cried out, "Please, leave me a light."

No answer came in response to her plea. She crawled from the cot and made her way to the window, feasting on the stars.

She dragged the cot under the window and sat so that the only things she could see were the pricks of light against the velvety sky. With her head against the hard brick behind her, she closed her eyes and prayed for sleep.

"What do you mean you arrested that girl?" Ma's hand paused in pouring Ward's coffee. "Has that job of yours blinded you to the good things of this world?"

"The evidence is stacked against her." Ward took the pot from her hand and filled his mug. "I know you're taken with her, but until I get to the bottom of this, Katie has to stay behind bars." The telegram he'd sent his boss ought to stall the marshal for a day or two, maybe longer.

He'd told them of Amos's alias. Once they found the man, they could get to the bottom of Katie's innocence.

"Bring her here. I'll watch her." Ma crossed her arms. "She could have run many times, Ward. Why stay in

Somerville after committing the crimes you say she committed? Why move from stealing poker money to robbing a bank? It doesn't make sense. There's another woman in town doing these things. Yes, bring Katie here. We'll put her to work."

"She tried to run."

"Of course she did. You frightened her."

Ward glanced at his father. "Help me out here, Pa."

"I learned a long time ago not to disagree with your mother when she's set on something."

Caroline came in the front door. "I hope you don't mind that I've come home tonight. I can't bear to stay at the hotel knowing Katie is behind bars."

Ward slapped the table. "You helped put her there."

"I know, but…I'm having second thoughts." She shrugged. "She's never given me reason to doubt her before."

"She has every one of you blinded by her charms." Ward shoved his seat back. He should have stayed in town. "I am not releasing her from jail."

"I think you will." Ma grinned and stood next to Caroline. "We know you care for her."

"My feelings don't matter here." Of course he cared for her. He'd been duped as well as anyone by her sweet personality and pretty face. He'd actually thought she might be the woman to make him want to settle down. How blind he'd been. He stared at the formidable force of his mother and older sister. "Fine. I'll see what I can do in the morning."

"You'll go now." Ma gave a determined nod. "The poor girl is probably frightened out of her mind and hungry to boot. Take that beast of a car and go fetch her."

Ward sighed and rolled the kinks from his shoulders. "This is the king of bad ideas." He grabbed his hat and stormed out of the house. He could lose his badge for this.

He glanced at the night sky. "God, I could use a double dose of help right about now."

After fighting to get the Ford started, he turned the car down the road and headed toward town. Clouds built to the north, promising rain before the night was over. He hoped it would wait until he returned home. Was that God's warning? That life around Katie would always be stormy?

He'd put her under house arrest at the farm, and then focus his attention on finding Amos and the rest of the bank robbers. If he found them, and a woman with them who resembled Katie, then he could put this whole mess behind him. He'd also owe Katie a huge apology if she were innocent, and that was a mighty big if.

He cut the ignition to the Ford and unlocked the door to the jail. After leaving the sheriff a note about his intentions, he lit a lantern and moved to the two cells the jail housed. His heart ached to see Katie propped against the wall under the one window. It had never occurred to him she might be afraid of the dark.

The jingle of the keys caused her to jerk awake. "Who's there?"

"Ward." He unlocked the door and held up the lantern as he stepped into the cell. "At my mother's request, I'm putting you under house arrest at the farm."

"I'm not going." She crossed her arms and turned her head.

"Why?" It had to be better than here, even with him living there.

"I don't want to be under the same roof as you." Her voice broke, cutting another piece out of his heart. "I'm fine where I am until you come to your senses."

"If I go back without you, Ma will have my hide."

"I hope it hurts."

He laughed. She sure was a spunky thing. "Regardless

of how you feel, you're coming with me. If you try to run, I'll shoot you."

"You probably would, too. You're that mean." She slid from the cot and stomped past him. Her hair had fallen from its updo and cascaded down her back in a wave of ebony.

He stuck his free hand in his pocket to keep from running his fingers through the strands. "The car is out front. Wait for me to lock up."

"Where's my deed?"

"In the sheriff's safe. Do you plan on stealing it back?"

She huffed and stormed outside as the first raindrops fell. "It's raining. Will your car make it in the rain?"

"We'd best hurry or it might be the wettest ride you've ever had." Door locked, he jogged to crank the car to life while Katie climbed into the front seat. He didn't know why he wasn't worried about her running or trying to drive away, but he wasn't. Could his mother be right and Katie was innocent in all this?

Car started, he climbed behind the wheel as the clouds released their burden. The Ford's headlights barely cut through the downpour. He drove at ten miles per hour. It would be a long ride with a passenger as cold as the wind blowing the rain.

"You won't be a guest," he told her. "You're still under arrest."

"I'll earn my keep," she said without looking at him. She wrapped her arms around her middle. "But don't expect a thanks for dragging me out here. I want as little to do with you as possible."

As much as he understood how she felt, her words hurt. Please, God, let him put an end to all the indecision and get on with his life. It pained him to know that even if innocent, Katie would not want to be a part of his future plans.

If guilty, the pain over her pulling the wool over his eyes would fade in time.

Skirting mud puddles, he drove the Ford into the yard and stopped inside the barn. He'd barely cut the ignition before Katie was marching toward the house, her mass of hair now a dark river down her back. A single light burned in the kitchen, showing that Ma had waited for them. Most likely to make sure he hadn't returned without Katie.

Katie stopped on the front porch and waited. Good. He didn't want her barging into the house before he had time to warn her that Caroline was home. He'd seen the look of despair cross her face when his sister had fired her.

After he'd shut the barn doors, he splashed his way to the porch. "There's something I need to warn you about."

She tilted her head. "More good news?"

He scratched his chin. She wouldn't take the information kindly. Not after his sister had turned her back on her. "Caroline is here, too."

Her face hardened like granite. She whirled and stormed into the rain.

"Where are you going?"

"Back to jail."

Chapter 19

Katie washed the breakfast dishes, setting a china plate in a drainer. Since she'd arrived at the farm, she had yet to speak to anyone. She may have slept in a comfortable bed, eaten a delicious meal of eggs and bacon with fresh flaky biscuits, but she was still a prisoner. She even wore someone else's clothes.

It had taken everything in her to accept the pale blue dress of Caroline's. The pain in the other woman's eyes, her apology, her desire to be called by her first name—none of it softened Katie's heart. She'd been arrested, fired and stripped of everything she had in a matter of hours.

She glanced out the kitchen window to where Ward and his pa did the morning chores. All of the pain she experienced was because of a handsome Ranger she'd let into her heart. He'd set his hook, and the barbs ripped with each betrayal. She tried to hang on to God's promises, the ones that said God was watching out for her and would never leave her, but it was sometimes harder than she could manage.

"This is the last of them." Lucy set some glasses on the sideboard. "I wish you'd speak to us. It was Ma and Caroline that convinced Ward to release you from jail. I was in bed or I would have fought for you, too."

Katie blinked back tears and swallowed the words that lodged in her throat. She couldn't allow herself to relax in Ward's home. The moment she let her guard down, something else would land on her shoulders. It wouldn't take much more to completely break her.

"Don't cry. Ward will fix everything." Lucy patted her shoulder. "He always does."

She wanted to say he'd fixed things just fine, but held her tongue and nodded instead in a vain attempt to placate the young girl. She set the glasses into the hot soapy water and continued her work. If she must stay under the traitor's roof, she'd work as hard, or harder, than any of them. Having grown up on a farm, she knew what needed doing without being told.

Caroline entered the kitchen, the bread basket in her hands, and tried to catch Katie's attention. Katie watched her out of the corner of her eye, but refused to acknowledge the other woman's presence.

Caroline sighed. "You're being ridiculous, Katie. I told you I was sorry and that you still have your job as soon as this is over. I'll do everything I can to make sure you're hired back. I spoke out of fear, yesterday. I made a mistake."

"You're the reason I'm here." Katie tossed the dishrag into the water, splashing her dress with suds. "You fell for the circumstantial evidence the same as anyone. After working with me six days a week, often for ten hours a day, you still believed me capable of such a crime." She stormed out the back door, letting it bang behind her.

She wanted to set off into the woods and find Amos. Once she did, she'd make him tell everyone she had nothing to do with the robbery. She'd force him at gunpoint if she had to. No, Ward had taken her gun.

Ignoring the glances of Ward and his father, she grabbed the basket from the side of the chicken coop and unlatched the gate. The chickens clucked and squawked as she dug under their warm bodies for the eggs. Solitary chores were the ones she preferred. Chores that left her to her own thoughts and allowed her to avoid questions.

When she emerged, Mrs. Alston was struggling to hang a quilt on the clothesline. Katie set the basket on a stump and went to help.

"Thank you. My arms aren't as strong as they once were and the girls are busy inside." Ma flashed a smile.

Katie nodded. She clipped a clothespin on the corner she held and then went to retrieve her basket. She desperately needed time with the Lord, but was afraid if she were to find a spot out of everyone's sight, they'd think she'd run off. What a mess.

After setting the eggs on the counter, she grabbed a feather duster and set out to dust every single room in the house. By the time she'd finished, she'd worked off most of her anger and dust bunnies dotted her hair. She plopped on the chintz sofa and rested her chin in her hands.

She needed to come to terms with her predicament. Silence wasn't the answer. Ma always said it was easier to draw a bear to honey than vinegar. Or was it a bee? Didn't matter. Either way, she needed to rethink her strategy. Ward's family felt guilty enough. Now, to convince them she was still the sweet Katie they'd known before. She'd make cookies.

Thirty minutes later, she set the first batch of oatmeal cookies on the counter. It felt good to bake again.

"Something smells good." Mrs. Alston stepped into the

kitchen. "There's nothing better than the aroma of fresh-baked cookies."

Katie forced a smile to her face. "I wanted to do something to pay you for your kindness in taking me in and getting me out of that awful jail."

Mrs. Alston's steps faltered. "You're no longer mad at us?"

"I'm still hurt, but I'm not one to wallow in pain or anger." Katie plucked two cookies off the tray and handed one to her.

Mrs. Alston chuckled. "Well played, my dear. Kill them with kindness. A ploy I've used myself many times. Don't worry. I won't let anyone in on your secret."

"I thought I was a better actress."

"According to my son, you're the best. After all, you pulled the wool over all of our eyes, according to him."

Katie bit into the chewy goodness. "You don't think so."

"I haven't thought you guilty for a second. Now, why don't you continue this charade by taking a plate out to the men? I'll watch the ones in the oven." She grinned.

Katie smiled, relieved that she'd found a willing conspirator.

Ward stopped mending the fence and watched as Katie strolled across the yard, a plate in her hands. She was a vision in one of Caroline's old dresses. While her hair was back in its usual updo, he preferred it the way it had been last night. Loose and flowing.

"I've brought cookies." She held the plate out, her smile forced and shaky.

"Why?" He wiped his hands on the thighs of his denim pants.

She shrugged. "I thought it the best thing to do, under the circumstances."

"Hmm." He quirked his mouth. Something else lurked in her mind. "Fishing for information?"

"Like what?" Her innocent look might have fooled him once upon a time, but no more.

"Like why I'm working on the farm and not out trying to find Amos."

"Since you brought it up, why don't you answer your own question?" She set the plate on the flat top of a post.

"I plan on laying low for a couple of days. I'm hoping by doing so, the bank robbers will grow bold again and come out of hiding."

"Sounds like a fair plan." She crossed her arms and stared at the horses. "I love to ride."

"Maybe I'll take you tomorrow." Now why did he offer to do a fool thing like that? Maybe he wasn't as averse to her charms as he tried to be. She smelled of lilac and oatmeal. A surprisingly pleasant scent. He took a deep breath before grabbing a cookie.

"You've been working hard."

She cut him a sideways glance. "I told you I wasn't afraid of hard work. You should know that by my prior occupation."

"Which one?"

"Be serious." She whirled on him faster than a cornered bobcat. "I'm trying to make pleasant conversation, and you want to play with words. You know good and well I'm talking of my job at the Harvey House."

He grinned around a mouthful of cookie. He had known what she was talking about, and, suspected crook or not, he enjoyed sparring with her. "Just checking."

"I should take the cookies back to the house."

He placed a hand over his heart. "Please don't. A hardworking man gets hungry."

"Humph. When I find a hardworking man, I'll let you

know." With a swish of her skirts, she headed back to the house.

Man, he loved that girl. Whoa. He choked on the cookie and ended up spitting it in the dirt. Love? No way. Impossible. *Lord, what have I gotten myself into?*

Pa exited the barn. "You all right, son? Are the cookies not any good? I've never known you to waste one before."

"Just choked."

"Yeah, a pretty gal will do that to you." Pa laughed.

Good grief, was he that transparent? "I'm in a quandary."

"That you are." Pa grabbed the last cookie on the plate. "It's a hard thing when a man is torn in two, as you seem to be. That gal's innocent, son. You got to prove it before something bad happens to her. You know deep in your heart she isn't capable of robbing banks and hurting people."

"I know." And he did. It became more imperative he find the real robbers and the dark-haired woman that looked like Katie. Although he knew in his heart she was innocent, the farm was still the safest place for her. Amos and his gang wouldn't dare try to get to her out here. Still, Ward needed to confront Amos.

Maybe the horse ride the next day would serve two purposes. One, to get Katie out of the house, and two, to draw the robbers out of hiding. If Amos was in the middle of it all, as Ward suspected, he might still have a hankering to do harm to Katie.

The thought sent a chill down his spine. Taking her away from the safety of the farm could be a mistake. Using her as bait could be very dangerous.

Sure, he told Pa he believed her innocent, but there was still that annoying gnat of doubt that buzzed around his head. If he could shut out the thoughts whirling through his head, he could think more clearly. Taking Katie riding could also give her a chance to escape. He'd have to make sure not to let his guard down.

He hammered another nail into the fence, feeling a bit as if he were putting a nail into his coffin. Helping Pa around the farm had him confused almost as much as his feelings for Katie. The lure of being a Ranger faded with each day he stayed in Somerville. Add in the fact he could still feel the occasional twinge in his side from the gunshot, and he wasn't sure he wanted to go back. He had some serious soul-searching to do once he settled this case of the bank robbers and Katie.

He spent the rest of the time mending the fence in prayer. While he thought he knew what God was calling him to do, he still wasn't sure he was ready to take the step that would change his life. He'd been a Ranger for six years and was good at his job. But he was a good farmer, too.

By the time he'd finished, it was crowding lunchtime. He planned to spend the afternoon scouring the neighboring woods under the pretense of gathering firewood. By now, everyone in town would know Katie was staying at his place. While Ward thought it foolish, the robbers could very well come to the farm. Ward wanted to find them before they showed up.

After washing up in the bucket Ma kept outside the kitchen door for that purpose, he entered the kitchen to the aroma of baking ham. "I'm starved." He peered into the oven.

Ma flicked him with a dish towel. "You'll let the heat out. We're having sandwiches for lunch. Yours is on the table. That ham is for supper."

Ward sighed. If he did quit his job as a Ranger, he'd have to set to work building his own cabin right away. He knew just the spot, too. A pretty little place on the other side of the barn. Close enough to enjoy Ma's cooking, but far enough away to afford him a bit of privacy. He glanced to where Katie sliced pickles.

What would it be like to come home each evening to her pretty face?

Chapter 20

Despite her reservations about being alone with Ward, excitement raced through Katie's veins at the opportunity to get off the farm. She sped through the morning chores and donned an old riding costume of Caroline's. While the thought of Ward's sister's belief that Katie could be guilty, if even for a moment, still rankled, she'd stuck by her resolve to act kindly. After grabbing a picnic basket with food and water, she grabbed a battered leather hat from a coat rack and dashed to the barn.

Ward paused in saddling a pretty chestnut mare with a white blaze down her nose. "You're anxious this morning."

"It'll be good to be on the back of a horse again." She hadn't ridden since leaving home. She spotted her pistol tucked into his waistband next to his gun. Was he expecting trouble?

"This is Lovely. She's a sweet-tempered horse and shouldn't give you any trouble." He handed her the reins and took the basket. "We'll ride up the mountain awhile before stopping for lunch. I hope you aren't too out of practice. We'll be gone most of the day."

"I'm looking forward to it." She held her breath as he placed his hands around her waist and helped her into the saddle. She shouldn't allow his touch to affect her. Regardless of how she felt about him, knowing he thought her capable of robbery showed that Ward didn't know her at all. It was best that her heart get resigned to the fact there could be nothing between her and Ward.

Ward led a big white horse from the barn, Katie following on Lovely. He swung into the saddle and waved to his mother, who watched from the porch. With a tug on his hat, he led the way around the barn and into the trees.

Leaves fell from the trees and crunched under the horses' hooves. Katie breathed deep of pine needles and brisk autumn air. She'd let her hat hang around her neck by its rawhide string and had settled back into her saddle. She squinted against the sun blinking through the tree branches.

Ma used to say that one was closer to God when outside. On beautiful days like this, Katie believed her.

They rode along a babbling brook, until Ward found a place to cross. He scanned the ground on each side of them, and had yet to say a single word since they'd left the house. What was he looking for? Was the invitation for a day out a ruse to uncover more information? Katie scowled. She'd enjoy the day despite his silence. Who wanted to carry on a conversation with a grumpy man, anyway?

They veered across the creek, the silence so thick Katie could almost taste it. She couldn't take the suspense any longer. "What are you looking for?

Ward glanced over his shoulder. "Excuse me?"

"You're searching for something. What is it?"

He sighed. "Tracks."

"You're looking for Amos." Prickles ran up and down

Katie's arms as she scanned the trees. "You're using me as bait."

His mouth clamped shut, and he turned back around. Katie had half a mind to turn around and head back to the farm. She didn't want to be dangled like a worm on a hook.

"I want to go back." The peace of the day was shattered as effectively as if a bullet had pierced it.

"Shh." Ward continued on.

He expected Katie to follow like an obedient puppy. Since she wasn't sure she could find her way back to the farm alone, she had no choice. Her shoulders tensed, waiting for a bullet to strike.

The horses continued on their way as if danger didn't lurk behind the next bush. That was good, right? The horses would alert them if someone came close. Why hadn't they brought Ward's dog?

Katie held the reins tight enough to cut into the palms of her hands. If she got shot, she'd take her pistol out of Ward's waistband and use it on him. "I want my gun."

"Nope."

"You're expecting trouble. I'm a good shot." She hated the whine in her voice. "Can we stop? I'm hungry."

Ward sighed and reined his horse to a halt, then backed it up until he was side by side with Katie. He glared at her with those remarkable hazel eyes. No, she would not think that way. Handsome is as handsome does, and Ward was acting ugly.

"Yes, I'm trying to draw Amos out of hiding. You have something he wants."

"But it's in the safe."

"He doesn't know that."

True, but Katie didn't have to like it.

"So unless you want to alert him to our presence, if he's even around here, I'd appreciate it if you'd stop talking."

She nodded and slapped her hat on her head as if it could

protect her. Keeping her eyes trained on Ward's back, she willed him to turn back. If they ran across Amos and his gang, she doubted whether they'd leave alive. Amos would shoot first, and then search for the deed. After robbing the bank, he had nothing else to lose and a lot to gain by ridding the earth of Katie Gamble.

Ward's stomach rumbled. If he was hungry, Katie must be, too. As much as he hated to stop, the horses could also use a rest. "We'll stop here for half an hour before another hour's ride. Then, if we don't find anything, we'll head back."

"I hope we don't find anything." Katie slid from the saddle. "I don't relish getting shot." She took the basket from the back of Ward's horse and took a seat on a fallen log.

Ward didn't want to get shot either. That particular experience was growing old. If they did find Amos, and gunfire was exchanged, he'd have to give Katie her gun and pray she didn't train it on him. His gut told him she wouldn't, but there was still that niggling idea that she wasn't innocent. And he hated the thought.

He knew the idea wasn't from God yet he couldn't let go. Too many years of not trusting other people had him holding on to her guilt like a lifeline. He pulled her pistol from his waistband. It was time to let go of the line. "Here."

"Really? You aren't afraid I'll shoot you and run to freedom?" Her mouth quirked as she tucked the pistol into the top of her boot.

"No." He took a deep breath. "I'm not. I have a confession. I believe you're innocent, Katie. I've done a lot of thinking since you've been at the farm. I've seen you with my family. I can't believe you're a cold-blooded robber."

"Thank you." Tears shimmered in her eyes. "Then why take me to the farm? Why arrest me?"

God forgive him. "To draw Amos out of hiding, mostly, although I do think you're safer away from town."

She hung her head and fiddled with the paper wrapped around a sandwich. "You brought me out here to protect me?"

"Mainly." He sat next to her and hung his hands between his legs. "You might have been safe in jail, but I would have to come home at some point, leaving you unguarded. There's still this niggling doubt that I'm a fool, lured by your pretty face. But my heart tells me my mind is tied in knots." Much like his stomach. "I'm trained to look at the evidence."

"Which points to me." She handed him a sandwich, then unscrewed the top to the canteen. He tried not to watch her slender throat as she swallowed, her hair falling free of its updo and falling down her back. That's how he liked seeing her most—her hair falling free.

He clutched the sandwich in order to keep himself from running his fingers through the strands. Caroline's riding costume was a bit tight in some places and short in others. While it still covered Katie modestly, it emphasized the curves she had that his sister didn't. They should never have stopped for lunch. If they'd stayed on the horses, his mind wouldn't be wandering into dangerous territory.

"I appreciate your wanting to keep me safe, but you should have told me." She turned her dark eyes on him. "Admit it. Until you brought me to the farm, you thought I might be guilty. Something changed in the last twenty-four hours and not before."

"You're right. When I arrested you, the evidence seemed to be against you. It still does. It wasn't until I took the time to think through things, to pray about it, that I realized I was wrong the whole time. I'm sorry for hurting you."

High spots of color appeared on her cheeks, showing she still held on to the pain and anger, if only a little. He couldn't blame her. He had done her a grave injustice. One he intended to rectify with a telegram to his boss the moment he went back to town.

"Apology accepted," she said. "From this moment forward, we're two people working toward the same goal—the goal of seeing Amos Moore, or whatever his name is, behind bars." She held out her hand.

He returned the shake. "Agreed." The burden he'd been carrying lifted from his shoulders, making him freer than he'd been since first setting eyes on Katie. He finished unwrapping his sandwich and sank his teeth into ham and cheese between two thick pieces of homemade bread.

They ate in companionable silence, something Ward realized they'd never done before. He'd always been questioning, she'd always been on the defensive. He enjoyed it and came to realize that Katie had a marvelous sense of humor. He laughed more in the thirty minutes they took for lunch than he had all year.

When they'd finished, they both squatted beside the creek to wash their hands. He splashed Katie's face. She shrieked and fell backward, landing on her backside. "That's freezing." She splashed him back until they were both damp and shivering.

"We'd better get into the sunshine before we catch pneumonia." He held out his hand, relishing the feel of hers. He helped her back onto Lovely. When they'd left the barn that morning, he wanted only to get through the day and find what he'd been looking for. Now he realized he'd been looking for Katie. Now that he had found her, he didn't want the day to end.

Instead of her following behind, they rode side by side. Ward still glanced around the trail as they rode, but headed back the way they'd come instead of going farther from home. Maybe Amos had left town after all.

Ward had telegraphed his boss after the robbery, so he

knew others were also looking for the man. He studied Katie's profile, admiring the smooth curve to her cheek, the straight nose, the full lips and lashes that brushed her skin when she blinked. She caught him staring and faced him, her smile jolting his heart.

"Isn't this better than constant disagreement?" she asked.

He chuckled. "Definitely."

His horse nickered and tossed his head. Ward glanced over his shoulder. The sensation of being watched prickled his skin. Not wanting to alarm Katie, he moved his horse closer to hers. "Tell me about this land you love so much."

"It's fertile mountain land. You can grow almost anything under the sun. There's a beautiful creek that runs just past the cabin." Her face lit up as she spoke of the place she loved so much. "Ma and Pa are both buried there. I don't really care about the oil." She flicked him a sideways glance. "It's the sentimental things that matter."

"I understand. That's how I feel about our farm, too."

Her horse neighed and skipped sideways. Katie patted the animal's neck and spoke in soothing tones. "It's all right, girl. We'll be out of the woods soon enough." She glanced over her shoulder, and then bent and pulled her pistol from her boot. "Then we can ride like the wind."

"You know someone's back there?" Ward should have known he couldn't fool her for a minute.

"Yes. I also know we can't run with all these trees." She clicked for Lovely to pick up the pace.

A shot rang out. Katie fell from her horse.

Chapter 21

Katie crawled into the bushes to the sound of Ward's harsh whisper. "I'm fine. I'm fine. I'm fine." If she said the words enough, chanted them like a mantra, she might be able to take her mind off the fire burning through her shoulder. She clutched her pistol like a lifeline. She suddenly missed the routine of working for the Harvey Company, where each day was the same.

She scooted against a tree trunk and closed her eyes. A crashing through the brush had her on her knees, gun pointed. She'd known all along Amos wouldn't give up. Even if he didn't want the land, he didn't like being thwarted. Katie had rejected him, violently, leaving a reminder on his cheek. The man might want revenge for the slight more than for the deed.

"It's me." Ward burst from the brush and to her side. "Where are you hit?"

"My shoulder. But I think it's just a graze."

He ran his hands over her and nodded. "Stay close."

As if she had other ideas. She kept as close to him as she could without stumbling over his feet. Adrenaline coursed through her, pushing the pain away.

Ward reached behind him and grasped her hand. The gesture calmed her, a promise that everything would be all right. She brushed the hair from her eyes and fought to stay focused.

"Do you see anything?"

He shook his head. They took refuge in some tall grass. "The horses bolted. I'm hoping they'll come back, but we may have to walk out of here. Are you up to it?"

"Yes." She'd do whatever it took to get back to the farm alive. She stared at the gun in her hand. She would even pull the trigger on another human being if she had to. Hopefully, she wouldn't have to. She was a good shot, but other than the feet of the men in the woods, she'd never shot at anything but targets and food for the table. Nausea threatened to choke her.

She glanced at Ward's strong profile. Could she do it to save him? She thought so. Oh, Lord, please don't test the theory.

Ward ripped the sleeve from his shirt and tied it around Katie's wound. She hissed and closed her eyes as he increased pressure. "I'm sorry. You're a real trouper, Katie. I might make you an honorary Texas Ranger."

"No, thanks." She opened her eyes.

He smiled down at her and cupped her cheek. "Stay with me."

"I'll do my best." It was getting harder to concentrate. She stared at the bare tree branches, letting the cool breeze kiss her flushed cheeks. Where was the shooter? Why wasn't he coming close enough for Ward to take him out? She wanted to go to sleep.

Ward patted her cheek. "Stay awake."

"I can't believe you thought me a dangerous criminal

when a little bit of blood makes me queasy." She plucked at the bloody sleeve of the blouse she wore and grimaced.

"It's more than a little blood," he muttered. "You've been shot. Can you move?"

She nodded. Anything was better than staying still and waiting to be found.

Ward put his arm around her waist and her good arm over his shoulder. Together, they moved as fast as she could through the forest. Each step was agony to her burning shoulder, and she wanted to beg him to stop, but doing so would only make them easier to see. She gritted her teeth and persevered on, thankful for Ward's strength.

A twig snapped. Ward froze, putting a finger to Katie's lips. When the sound didn't come again, they continued on, stopping only to take a few sips of water from the canteen slung around Ward's shoulder.

Katie's head pounded and sweat poured down her back despite the autumn day. Trudging through the forest in pain was the hardest thing she'd ever had to do. She'd never complain about grumpy customers or rolling silverware again. "I need to rest."

Ward set her under a pine tree. Worry lines creased his face. "I'm sorry for dragging you out here. It was a stupid idea."

"No, it wasn't. We were caught by surprise, is all. Your mother will have me as good as new once we return." She forced a shaky smile. "It's just a graze, Ward. I'll live."

"I hate seeing you in such pain." He pressed his lips against her forehead. "You're burning up."

"It is rather warm for fall, isn't it?"

"It's not the weather." He sighed and sat back, his hands dangling over his knees. "Maybe I should leave you here and go look for the horses."

"No!" She gripped his shirt. "You can't leave me." Fear

choked her. If he left her alone, she'd die. The shooter would find her and finish her off.

"All right." He rubbed his hands over his face. "In all my years as a Ranger, I've never been in this predicament."

"Saddled with a female?"

He gave her a crooked grin. "Yes. I've always been holed up with men who could take care of themselves."

"I can take care of myself." She glared and pushed to her feet. "Let's go."

"Are you sure? You look kind of wobbly."

She shoved aside a branch and let it swing back. Ward chuckled and dodged it before the branch could slap him. She'd show him who could take care of themselves. She bit her lip against the pain and trudged in the direction she thought was the farm. How long would they have to be gone before someone came for them?

Her emotions ran the gamut from being angry at Ward for putting her in danger to being glad he was there to urge her on. She could think of better ways to spend time with the man she loved. She could finally allow herself to admit that she loved him. That was why it had pained her so much when he didn't trust her and had arrested her.

Now she could see his misguided attempt at keeping her safe. Her lip curled. A lot of good it did. Here they were, trudging through the woods, and night would be falling soon. She shook her head and continued on, praying for God to help them find a way out.

A bullet slammed into the tree next to her head. She shrieked and ducked, banging her wounded shoulder against the tree trunk. Blackness consumed her.

Ward whirled, shooting off three rounds from his revolver. A man cried out.

"Katie!" Ward scrambled through the leaves to her side. He patted her cheek. He'd pushed her too hard, relied on her stubbornness to goad her into continuing when she was plainly exhausted. And now the shooter had made another attempt on her life. What had he done?

"I'm fine." Her eyes snapped open. "I hit my shoulder. I'm going to throw up." She rolled over and lost her lunch.

"I think I got him. I need to go check. Stay here." He hated leaving her, but it was the only way. She'd never be quick enough to get away if the man was still alive. Not in her condition.

"Hurry back." She closed her eyes. "Although, this pile of leaves is very comfortable. I think I love them."

Goodness, she was delirious. Ward rushed, bent over, to where he'd fired his shots. Maybe Katie had lost more blood than he thought. What if she died out there? He'd never forgive himself. He'd finally found a woman he wanted to spend the rest of his life with, and he could very well have gotten her into a situation that would get her killed.

Making as little noise as possible on the leaf-strewn path, Ward approached the man he'd shot. Amos Moore lay on his back, blood soaking his leather vest. Two of Ward's shots had taken the man in the gut. He shook his head. The man may have been a cold-blooded crook, but Ward hated taking even his life.

He glanced around the area. Where were the rest of the robbers? Had they skipped town right after the robbery? Was Amos so set on taking what belonged to Katie that he'd stuck around while the others left?

Ward took note of where the body lay and hurried back to Katie. She was sitting and fiddling with the bandage around her wound. She glanced up with a question in her eyes.

"Amos is dead," Ward said, holding out a hand to help her to her feet. "The others must have left town."

She sighed. "How desperate he must have been to want

the land that badly, because he wanted to make me pay for rejecting him."

Now they'd never know his motives. Regardless that the man was dead, Ward was relieved that the danger to Katie was now past. He'd ride into town the next day and let his boss know what had happened. The case was closed. There was nothing more to do than to make a decision that would affect the rest of his life.

"Can you make it back?" He slipped his arm around her waist. "Lean on me."

"I'll go as far as I can."

She had spunk, no denying it. The sun was starting to set behind the trees, casting the woods into a deeper shadow. He couldn't spend the night alone with Katie. What would people say, not to mention that predators walked the paths at night?

She leaned heavily on him, her breathing growing heavier with each step. He needed to leave her and go for help, but that would leave her at the mercy of the elements and wild animals. Having her walk all the way home was asking too much. He prayed for help.

"I can't keep going." She sagged against him. "I'm tired."

He helped her sit. He cupped her face and tucked her hair behind her ears. "It's getting colder, Katie. We have to keep moving."

"Leave me." Defeat laced her words.

"I won't." He studied the bandage. The bleeding had stopped. He helped her take a drink from the canteen and shook the small amount left. He'd go without. It wasn't the first time.

He stood and studied their surroundings. Unless he was mistaken, the woods ended a few yards in front of them and they'd enter into the meadow. They were only a couple of miles from home. "Come on. We're almost there."

"No. Go get help."

"You are a stubborn woman, Katie Gamble." He scooped her into his arms, determined to carry her the rest of the way.

She closed her eyes and rested her head on his shoulder. The poor thing had no strength left.

His legs trembled by the time they cleared the trees. He grinned. The horses they'd ridden what seemed like weeks ago were waiting. His horse had gotten the reins tangled around a dead tree and Lovely had stuck by its side. "Sweetheart, our ride is here."

He helped her onto the back of his horse, untangled the reins and then swung into the saddle behind her. Lovely would follow. By the light of the moon and stars, they headed home. Soft snores emanated from Katie and Ward tightened his grip. Soon, she'd be snug in bed with Ma fussing over her.

God had watched over them, giving them strength when needed. Ward kissed the top of Katie's tangled hair. He didn't plan on ever letting her go. While the horses plodded toward home, Ward's head bobbed as he struggled to keep his eyes open.

The day had taken a toll on them both. He'd drowsed in the saddle many times over the years, but never with someone in his lap. He couldn't sleep now and risk her falling from the horse. He bit the insides of his cheeks, praying the momentary pain would keep him awake.

A light bobbed across the meadow. Ward squinted when another one blinked to life. Help had arrived. He spurred the horses faster.

"Son, we were mighty worried." Pa held up the lantern. "What happened?"

"We ran into one of the bank robbers. Katie took a graze to the shoulder."

"Best we get her home in a hurry." Pa turned and sprinted for the house.

"Honey, we're home." Ward urged the horse into a jog, lured by the light in the kitchen window.

"The poor thing." Ma held the door open as Ward slid from the horse and gathered Katie into his arms. "Get her straight upstairs to bed so I can take care of her."

Ward followed Ma's instructions, placing Katie on top of the coverlet as if she were a china doll. He leaned over and grazed her lips with his.

Chapter 22

Katie stepped into the dining room of the hotel and smoothed the skirt of her new uniform. While her arm still ached when she lifted something heavy, she was more than happy to get back to work.

"I'm so glad you aren't a crook." Sarah rushed to give her a hug. "I thought for sure I'd be arrested for sneaking you that sandwich."

"Don't worry about it. Thankfully, it was all a huge misunderstanding." Katie met Ward's gaze over the other girl's shoulder.

Katie's cheeks heated. Life couldn't be better, and the future looked brighter still. While she had qualms about a relationship with a man involved in a dangerous profession, her heart couldn't help but beat faster every time she laid eyes on him. Each glance, each touch of his hands, left her feeling like a child at Christmas.

Caroline, Miss Alston as Katie called her during work hours, patted her shoulder on her way past. "It's good to have you back." She carried a stack of mail in her hand. "Six more weeks on your contract. How does that make you feel?"

"Conflicted." If she renewed her contract, she'd be obliged to work another six months. If she didn't sign a new contract, what would she do with her life? She glanced again at Ward. He held the key to her decision.

The woman who had once sat at a table with Amos sashayed into the room, took a look around and then sat at Katie's table. Today, she wore the infamous yellow dress. Katie swallowed against the lump in her throat. If the woman was a crook, as Katie suspected, why was she still in town? Was she so brazen as to think she wouldn't get caught?

Katie made her way to Ward. "I believe that is the woman who has been stealing from people at the saloons."

He peered over his coffee cup. "Yeah, I've been watching her for the last couple of days. A few men have come forward as witnesses. Go ahead and serve her. Don't make her suspicious."

Katie nodded and headed over to take the woman's order. "How may I serve you this morning?"

"Just tea and toast, please." The woman unfolded a newspaper and held it in front of her face. "Remember the gentleman I sat with a few weeks back?"

Katie's hand trembled as she turned the cups on the table to their right format in order to alert the drink girl as to what the customer wanted. "Yes, ma'am. I haven't seen him in a while."

"Pity." She sighed. "I had business to discuss with him. I'm leaving town on the next train and wanted to return something of his. Turns out that it's quite worthless."

The forged deed most likely. "I'll give him the message if I see him." Katie rushed to the kitchen, returning only moments later with the woman's toast. The woman ate a few bites, then left.

Ward gave Katie a nod and followed the stranger. Katie's shoulders relaxed. The woman could be the final link in the chain that had kept Katie a prisoner for so long. Finally, things could truly be over. Maybe she'd go home for a visit. Check out the home place and decide whether to keep the land or sell. If only Ward would tell her of his plans, then she could make hers.

"Could you follow me to the kitchen?" Caroline appeared at her side, a sad look on her face.

"Have I done something wrong?" Katie clutched at her throat.

"No, nothing like that." Caroline led the way through the kitchen and out the back door. She handed Katie an envelope. Tears appeared in the head waitresses eyes. "You're being transferred to New Mexico. A girl broke her contract and they need an immediate replacement. You leave on the next train."

Katie's hand shook as she took the offending paper. "Transferred?" It couldn't be. She wouldn't see Ward for weeks.

"I'm sorry, but there's nothing I can do. Hurry and pack." Caroline gave her a quick hug. "The train leaves in less than an hour."

Legs wooden and heart numb, Katie headed to her room to change and pack. A few items of clothing had been donated by the kind ladies of the church after the fire, but her wardrobe still lacked anything suitable for travel. She donned the brown split skirt of Caroline's old riding costume and grabbed a pale blue blouse from a hook on the wall. So very different from the yellow dress that had disappeared while she was behind bars.

Dressed, she rolled the other few remaining items, along with two uniforms, into a battered cardboard suitcase, and then took one last look around the room she'd shared with Sarah. There wasn't time to say goodbye…to anyone. *Oh, Lord, please let Ward be outside.* She could write to her friend, but she wanted to tell the man she loved goodbye in person.

She blinked back tears and made her way downstairs and to the street. Ward was nowhere to be seen. The train whistle blew, and Katie hurried. She prayed he'd understand her leaving without seeing him once Caroline gave him the news.

On the train platform, she turned in slow circle, not giving up hope that she'd catch one last glimpse of him. When the conductor called for all to board, she straightened her shoulders and boarded.

She chose a seat beside the window and leaned her forehead against the glass. As the train pulled away, she caught a glimpse of Ward running alongside. She placed her hand flat as if she could touch him, and watched until the train picked up speed, leaving her heart behind.

"Where is Katie going?" Ward burst into the restaurant. "Why did she leave without saying a word?"

Caroline turned slowly, her face pale. "She got an immediate transfer. I'm sorry."

"Where is she going?"

"New Mexico."

He needed to intercept the train. Locking up the woman in yellow hadn't taken but minutes. Neither had sending the telegram telling his boss that the other robbers were holed up in San Antonio. The case was closed as far as Ward was concerned.

The next stop was an hour down the line. If he rented a horse from the livery instead of heading home first, he could ride like the wind and hopefully, God willing, arrive at the next town before the train left. He'd searched his entire life for a woman like Katie. He didn't intend for her to get away.

"Tell Ma and Pa I won't be home for supper." He dashed outside and down the street to the livery. What he would do once he found her, he wasn't sure. She still had over a month on her contract, and she wasn't the type of woman to break something binding. He had a bit of money saved. He'd stay with her until her contract was up. There was nothing holding him in Somerville. He'd telegrammed his resignation that morning.

He handed over the funds for the fastest horse in the livery and galloped out of town. With no coat or hat, no provisions, he rode like a madman, his mind set on one thing, and that was getting to Katie.

Prayers flowed from his lips like water through a sieve. Where would they be if he'd taken the time to pray in the beginning? If he'd stopped to ask God about Katie's innocence and then actually stopped to listen? She still wouldn't have broken her contract, of that he was certain, but he knew in his heart she would have married him when it expired. He planned on asking her the moment he saw her again.

The horse's hooves pounded, its long legs eating up the miles as Ward kept it following the tracks. He'd slow its pace occasionally, in order not to overtax the poor beast, but would soon urge it on again.

As he neared town, he passed other travelers on the road, all of them leaping out of his way. He reached the train station as the train was pulling away. No! He raced the horse toward the train. If he got close enough, he could board from the animal's back.

He pulled closer to the last car and leaned, his fingers brushing against the iron railing. "Come on." He urged the horse closer. A young boy watched with an open mouth.

"Watch my horse for me," Ward yelled. He lunged, wrapping his arms around the railing and kicking his leg over.

The horse slowed, finally coming to a stop. The boy took the reins and stared after the train. Ward waved then ducked into the first car. He hurried down the aisle, scanning every face for a dark-haired beauty. He located her in the second car from the front. He leaned against the seat and struggled to catch his breath.

"You…left…without saying…goodbye."

She leaped to her feet and threw her arms around his neck. "You came for me. But how?"

"Crazy fool leaped off the back of a horse," a man in the seat behind her said. "Just like a circus performer. He must love you a lot."

"Do you?" She cupped his cheek.

"With all my heart." He gathered her into a fierce hug, breathing in the scent of lilac. "Marry me."

"I'm still under contract." She pulled back and stared into his face. "What about your job?"

"I quit this morning." He grinned down at her. "Thought I'd give farming a try."

She took her bottom lip between her teeth and glanced at the approaching conductor. "I think you'd better purchase a ticket. It wouldn't do for a former Texas Ranger to be arrested as a stowaway."

Ward laughed and handed the conductor the money. He sat and pulled Katie down next to him. "You never answered me. Will you be my wife?"

"The minute my contract expires."

He pulled her close for a kiss, devouring her as a man half-starved. Clapping erupted around them, pulling him back to the present. "I guess this isn't the place, is it?"

Smiling, she shook her head. "What will you do for the next six weeks?"

He shrugged. "I haven't thought that far ahead. I've

some money saved, and I left a borrowed horse back at the last town. There are some loose ends to clean up. I'll get my affairs in order while you work."

He kept his arm around her shoulders, and closed his eyes as she laid her head on his chest. Nothing would part them again. Not a job, not an uncertain future about where they would live, nothing. Although, he believed he might just know where she wanted to live, and if he could, he'd find a way to give it to her as a wedding present. While she worked, he'd take a short trip to finalize some things.

"I love you." He kissed the top of her head.

"That's good, because I'd hate for my love not to be returned." She smiled into his face. "I do believe I may be marrying the craziest man in the state of Texas."

He laughed. "No doubt about it."

Chapter 23

Katie stood in front of the newly constructed Harvey House in Belen, New Mexico. She shaded her eyes in an attempt to locate Ward. He'd been gone for two weeks. Her heart sat heavy, weighing down her spirit. One week left on her contract and her fiancé was nowhere to be seen.

Life wasn't how she'd planned it. She'd given up on moving back to Missouri, having put the land up for sale shortly after arriving in New Mexico. The money would provide the funds for the improvements Ward wanted to make to the farm. She wouldn't need the land after marrying Ward. He was all she needed. She'd be perfectly happy living on his family farm. Hopefully her mother would have agreed with her decision to sell. The land had been in her family's hands for generations.

Oh, where was that man? He'd told her before leaving that he had loose ends to tie up, but that he wouldn't be gone more than a week, two at the most. Well, today marked two weeks and a day.

"He'll be back." Miss Lester, the head waitress, patted Katie's shoulder. "Men in love always come back."

Katie nodded. "I hope so. We're heading back to Texas the day my contract ends." She smiled at the thought of the wedding dress she'd spent her evenings sewing. It was loose and flowing with a long veil of silk rosettes at the crown; she wanted to stun her husband-to-be speechless.

A horse trotted past the hotel. The elderly cowboy on its back tipped his hat in her direction. Katie nodded, and then turned to head to the dormitory. A few more adjustments and her wedding dress would be complete. All she needed now was her groom.

What if Ward had confronted the last of the bank robbers that needed rounding up? He'd told her his boss needed his help, and since Katie had to fulfill her contract, Ward had seen no reason to say no. What if he lay somewhere bleeding from a fatal bullet?

Her blood drained to her feet. She shook her head. No need to borrow trouble. Ward knew what he was doing and was good at his job. Why else would he be needed? He'd been held up, that was all.

Relieved to find her room empty, she sat on the edge of her bed and prayed. Since the demise of Amos and all that the trouble with him had entailed, Katie was able to more easily see God's hand in it all. Ma would have told her it was always easy to hear God when things were going good; it was when they were bad that a person really needed to lean on His broad shoulders.

Katie bowed her head. She intended to do just that. Worrying would bring her nothing but stress. God would watch out for Ward.

The wedding dress hung from a hook on the wall. Yards of satin and lace. Katie would finish it that night and take her mind off the waiting. God willing, she'd lay eyes on Ward in the morning.

She smiled. If someone would have told her six months ago she'd fall in love with a Texas Ranger she would have told them they were crazy. A lot of things had changed since then. Katie was no longer a fugitive running from a thief. She was no longer a wanted woman having to hide. Out of all the terror and turmoil, God had given her a man to love. A man in a million.

She got up and ran her hand over the dress, remembering the last one she'd sewed. The infamous yellow dress that had caused so much suspicion. Maybe she'd wear yellow flowers, if she could find them. Flowers would be hard to find for a winter wedding, but maybe they could be ordered from a town farther south.

By the time she tied off the last knot on the hem of the dress, the clock gonged ten times. Katie hung the dress back on the hook so the wrinkles could fall out, and then climbed into bed.

Her roommate, Lilly, rushed into the room. "Just made it." The perky redhead flounced on her bed. "This town is full of men. I shouldn't have a bit of trouble finding myself one. You—" she grinned and pointed at Katie "—found the best of them all."

Katie returned her smile. "I brought him with me."

"Maybe I'll ask to be transferred to Texas." Lilly slid from the bed and disrobed to slip into her nightgown. "I hate to be a statistic, leaving the Harvey Company to get married, but there are so many eligible men, it's very hard to resist."

"I imagine it is." Katie pulled the blankets up to her chin, thankful she wasn't searching for a husband. She'd thought marriage was a faraway prospect. Now she would be Mrs. Ward Alston in a week's time. She didn't think she could wait that long.

Maybe they could marry before heading to Texas. No, Ma Alston would skin them both if they denied her the pleasure of a wedding. The letter Katie had received the day before said Ma Alston and Caroline would handle all the details. All Katie and Ward had to do was show up.

"You have that dreamy look on your face again," Lilly said. "Thinking of your wedding?"

"Aren't I always?" Katie giggled.

"The dress is beautiful. You're a fine seamstress." Lilly turned down the lamp. Her blankets rustled as she climbed into bed. "Will it be a large wedding?"

"I have no idea. My in-laws are handling all the details. I don't even know where the ceremony will be held."

"Lucky girl. What a wonderful surprise you'll have."

That it would be. Katie snuggled deeper into her covers against the evening chill. Since Pa was gone, she'd head down the aisle, alone, to meet Ward. No, not alone. God would be at her side, the Father to give her hand in marriage.

She fell asleep with dreams of Ward and the perfect wedding.

Ward settled onto the bench seat on the train, the leather creaking under his weight. It had been a long journey, but the last of the robbery gang were rounded up, and Ward carried a special surprise in his pocket for Katie.

Leaning his head against the window, he watched the fields rush past. Meadows full of cows sped past in a panoramic view. Train might be the fastest way to travel, but it wasn't fast enough for him. His journey had taken longer than anticipated. He'd sent Katie a telegram that morning in hopes she'd be at the train station to greet him. He'd missed her.

In five days they'd head home. In seven, they'd be husband and wife. Life couldn't be any sweeter.

A woman in blue cast him flirtatious glances from across the aisle. Ward pulled his hat lower across his eyes in the pretense of catching a nap. The last thing he wanted was to be drawn into conversation with a woman who would want what he wouldn't give. The only female company he wanted was Katie's.

It was astonishing that she'd fallen in love with him after all he'd put her through. Deep down, Ward had always believed her innocent, yet he'd let the power of his job cloud his thinking. That action had almost gotten his beloved killed. The thought still chilled him to the bone.

The sight of her falling from her horse after being shot still haunted his sleep. Only waking up next to her each morning for the rest of their lives would erase the image. She'd persevered like a trouper to follow him out of the woods. He couldn't think of a better woman to work side by side with him as they made a life for themselves and their future family.

God had indeed blessed him.

He woke to the sound of steam hissing from under the train as it pulled into the station. He scanned the faces on the platform, looking for one in particular. Only one woman stood dressed in Harvey waitress garb. Ward grinned and grabbed his suitcase from an overhead bin.

Clutching the worn leather, he excused himself multiple times and rushed down the aisle of the railroad car. When she caught sight of him, Katie squealed and dashed toward him.

Ward dropped his case and swept her into his arms, covering her face with kisses before slowing to claim her lips. Sweet nectar. He tightened his hold until she protested he was squeezing too hard.

"I can't help it. It is so good to see you." He smiled into her upturned face.

"I second that." She caressed his cheek. "What took you so long?"

"Those robbers were hiding way up in the hills. We only

found them because one of them squealed. But I'm here now. That's the important thing." He retrieved his case. "The next thing, maybe even more important, is that I am no longer a Texas Ranger. I turned in my badge."

"Good." Katie slipped her arm through his. "The days have stretched so long without you. Although it wouldn't have stopped me from becoming your wife, I'm partial to you being home each night and not riding the trails."

"Ready to head home?"

"More than ready."

Ward escorted her back to the restaurant, reluctant to leave her so she could go back to work. "Which one is your table? I'm starving."

She laughed and set him at one near the kitchen. "The chef has a fabulous roast beef on the menu."

"Sounds perfect." He watched as she flitted from one customer to the next. The last two days of her contract would pass too slowly, but Thursday would come and they'd arrive home in time for their Saturday wedding.

Katie's skirt swayed like a bell, drawing his attention to her slim hips. Once she was free, he never wanted to see her in black again. Only bright colors would suit his love. He couldn't wait until the only man she served a meal to was him.

He pushed back jealousy as she grinned at a couple of men in suits. She was good at her job, and he reminded himself that she belonged to him and him alone. He was a lucky man. He nursed his cup of coffee after finishing his meal, reluctant to leave. After two weeks away, he wanted to feast his eyes on Katie for the rest of the day.

The head waitress, a pleasant middle-aged woman, passed his table and smiled. "Mr. Alston, won't you take a seat at the counter? We need this table, and I know you want to stay."

"Thank you, ma'am." Ward grabbed his hat from the

table and moved to the offered stool. Since it swiveled, he could watch Katie to his heart's content. He patted his pocket, hearing the crinkle of paper. Yes, Katie would be very pleased with her gift.

"Katie once told me she would love yellow flowers at her wedding." A red-haired girl refilled his coffee. "Just in case you can manage." She winked and moved down the counter.

Yellow flowers? The minx. He remembered the mix-up with the yellow dress as well as she did. He'd send a telegram home and see what Ma could come up with. If anyone could find flowers in the winter, it would be Ma.

He motioned to Katie that he would be back and set off to send the telegram. He would also need a suit to be married in and hoped the store at the end of the street would have one ready-made in his size. If not, he'd wear Pa's old one, but Katie deserved for him to look his best. He knew she'd been spending every spare minute on her wedding dress.

His boots thudded on the wood sidewalks, kicking dust over his already dirty boots. A bath and a shave would serve him well, too. Katie hadn't seemed to mind the dust from the trail, but he did. Ward marched into his boarding-house and ordered hot water sent to his room.

He was going to take Katie out to dinner to celebrate his return, and although it would take all his willpower not to let her in on his surprise for her, he wanted to give her an evening she wouldn't soon forget. Complete with ice cream at the local parlor.

Katie would never have a reason to regret marrying him.

Epilogue

The wedding was going to be held in the barn. Katie let the curtains in her bedroom fall back into place. Her hands shook. She and Ward had arrived on the farm yesterday and she'd been held a virtual prisoner in the house. She smiled. So different from the last time she'd been kept under surveillance.

"Oh, my dear, you look beautiful." Ma Alston entered the room, her hands folded under her chin. "Like a princess."

Katie twirled, the gown swishing around her ankles. "I feel like one."

"And I'm a lady in waiting." Caroline peered into the mirror, smoothing the skirt of the lavender dress she wore. "Ma, you did a fine job making my dress."

"Thank you for standing up with me." Katie grasped her soon-to-be sister's hands. "It means a lot."

"No more than the way I felt when you telegraphed asking me to." Caroline gave her a hug. "Are we ready?"

Katie nodded, her mouth going dry. "I'm nervous, but excited."

"You should see my son. The man can't be still to save his life." Ma laughed. "His father isn't much better. I'll head to the barn and have Lucy wave out the door when we're ready for you to enter. Let's pray first."

They held hands while Ma led them in a prayer asking for God's blessing on the coming union. When she'd finished, all three women had tears in their eyes. "I'm gaining another daughter today and couldn't be happier." She patted Katie's cheek. "You're the perfect match for my son. I do believe you will be able to keep him in line just fine."

"I'll do my best." Katie kissed the older woman's cheek. "Thank you for giving him to me."

"Oh, go on with you." Ma beamed and bustled out the door.

Katie linked her arm in Caroline's. "I hope my legs will hold me up."

"You'll catch one glimpse of my brother and be tempted to run to him. You'll be fine."

Together they made their way down the stairs and into the bright winter afternoon. No clouds marred the cerulean sky. Katie couldn't have asked for a better wedding day.

She licked her lips and waited around the corner of the barn for Lucy's signal. The soft music of a piano drifted through the open doors. She smiled. The Alston family had thought of everything to make her day special. She couldn't wait to see what they'd done inside the barn.

The flurry of the day before had sent her excitement to such a high level, she'd gotten little sleep that night. She doubted she'd sleep any better tonight. Her face heated, thinking of what was to come. Lord, let her be pleasing to her husband.

"It's time," Lucy hissed.

Katie nodded, and Caroline took her place in front of

Katie as Lucy thrust a bouquet of yellow silk roses into her hands. "Yellow?"

Caroline nodded. "Wait until you see inside. Ma had fun."

Tears sprang to Katie's eyes. She stepped forward as the wedding march played.

The barn was like a burst of sunshine. Yellow fabric draped from the rafters and the backs of mismatched chairs. Caroline held her own yellow rose. At the end of the aisle, Ward turned, resplendent in a new suit with a yellow rose in his lapel. How had they managed all this?

Katie took her first step toward Ward, then another, each step increasing in speed until she had to hold herself back to keep from running. *Thank You, God.*

Ward held out his hand and Katie placed her trembling one in his. "You're beautiful," he whispered.

"So are you."

He laughed and turned to face the minister. "I prefer handsome, but I accept the compliment."

Katie giggled and blinked back tears.

"Dearly beloved, we are gathered here today..."

She heard little of the ceremony, so focused was she on the tender look in Ward's sparkling eyes. He was hers. All hers.

"I now pronounce you husband and wife."

Ward lifted her veil and gathered her face in his hands. "My wife." He kissed her.

Her life couldn't be more perfect, and she couldn't wait to begin the new chapter. She was the wife of the man of her dreams and married into a family that would go to any lengths to make her feel welcome.

She wrapped her arms around his neck and, not caring what the guests would think, returned his kiss with all the emotions welling in her.

* * * * *

REQUEST YOUR FREE BOOKS!

2 FREE INSPIRATIONAL NOVELS
PLUS 2
FREE
MYSTERY GIFTS

Love Inspired

YES! Please send me 2 FREE Love Inspired® novels and my 2 FREE mystery gifts (gifts are worth about $10). After receiving them, if I don't wish to receive any more books, I can return the shipping statement marked "cancel." If I don't cancel, I will receive 6 brand-new novels every month and be billed just $4.74 per book in the U.S. or $5.24 per book in Canada. That's a savings of at least 21% off the cover price. It's quite a bargain! Shipping and handling is just 50¢ per book in the U.S. and 75¢ per book in Canada.* I understand that accepting the 2 free books and gifts places me under no obligation to buy anything. I can always return a shipment and cancel at any time. Even if I never buy another book, the two free books and gifts are mine to keep forever.

105/305 IDN F49N

Name	(PLEASE PRINT)

Address	Apt. #

City	State/Prov.	Zip/Postal Code

Signature (if under 18, a parent or guardian must sign)

Mail to the **Harlequin® Reader Service:**
IN U.S.A.: P.O. Box 1867, Buffalo, NY 14240-1867
IN CANADA: P.O. Box 609, Fort Erie, Ontario L2A 5X3

**Are you a subscriber to Love Inspired books
and want to receive the larger-print edition?
Call 1-800-873-8635 or visit www.ReaderService.com.**

* Terms and prices subject to change without notice. Prices do not include applicable taxes. Sales tax applicable in N.Y. Canadian residents will be charged applicable taxes. Offer not valid in Quebec. This offer is limited to one order per household. Not valid for current subscribers to Love Inspired books. All orders subject to credit approval. Credit or debit balances in a customer's account(s) may be offset by any other outstanding balance owed by or to the customer. Please allow 4 to 6 weeks for delivery. Offer available while quantities last.

Your Privacy—The Harlequin® Reader Service is committed to protecting your privacy. Our Privacy Policy is available online at www.ReaderService.com or upon request from the Harlequin Reader Service.
We make a portion of our mailing list available to reputable third parties that offer products we believe may interest you. If you prefer that we not exchange your name with third parties, or if you wish to clarify or modify your communication preferences, please visit us at www.ReaderService.com/consumerchoice or write to us at Harlequin Reader Service Preference Service, P.O. Box 9062, Buffalo, NY 14269. Include your complete name and address.

LIDIR13R

REQUEST YOUR FREE BOOKS!

2 FREE INSPIRATIONAL NOVELS
PLUS 2
FREE
MYSTERY GIFTS

Love Inspired

HISTORICAL

INSPIRATIONAL HISTORICAL ROMANCE

YES! Please send me 2 FREE Love Inspired® Historical novels and my 2 FREE mystery gifts (gifts are worth about $10). After receiving them, if I don't wish to receive any more books, I can return the shipping statement marked "cancel." If I don't cancel, I will receive 4 brand-new novels every month and be billed just $4.74 per book in the U.S. or $5.24 per book in Canada. That's a savings of at least 21% off the cover price. It's quite a bargain! Shipping and handling is just 50¢ per book in the U.S. and 75¢ per book in Canada.* I understand that accepting the 2 free books and gifts places me under no obligation to buy anything. I can always return a shipment and cancel at any time. Even if I never buy another book, the two free books and gifts are mine to keep forever.

102/302 IDN F5CY

Name	(PLEASE PRINT)	
Address		Apt. #
City	State/Prov.	Zip/Postal Code

Signature (if under 18, a parent or guardian must sign)

Mail to the **Harlequin® Reader Service:**
IN U.S.A.: P.O. Box 1867, Buffalo, NY 14240-1867
IN CANADA: P.O. Box 609, Fort Erie, Ontario L2A 5X3

Want to try two free books from another series?
Call 1-800-873-8635 or visit www.ReaderService.com.

* Terms and prices subject to change without notice. Prices do not include applicable taxes. Sales tax applicable in N.Y. Canadian residents will be charged applicable taxes. Offer not valid in Quebec. This offer is limited to one order per household. Not valid for current subscribers to Love Inspired Historical books. All orders subject to credit approval. Credit or debit balances in a customer's account(s) may be offset by any other outstanding balance owed by or to the customer. Please allow 4 to 6 weeks for delivery. Offer available while quantities last.

Your Privacy—The Harlequin® Reader Service is committed to protecting your privacy. Our Privacy Policy is available online at www.ReaderService.com or upon request from the Harlequin Reader Service.

We make a portion of our mailing list available to reputable third parties that offer products we believe may interest you. If you prefer that we not exchange your name with third parties, or if you wish to clarify or modify your communication preferences, please visit us at www.ReaderService.com/consumerchoice or write to us at Harlequin Reader Service Preference Service, P.O. Box 9062, Buffalo, NY 14269. Include your complete name and address.

LIHDIR13R

REQUEST YOUR FREE BOOKS!
2 FREE WHOLESOME ROMANCE NOVELS IN LARGER PRINT
PLUS 2
FREE
MYSTERY GIFTS

⁂⁂⁂⁂⁂⁂⁂⁂⁂⁂⁂⁂⁂⁂⁂⁂⁂⁂⁂⁂⁂

HEARTWARMING™

⁂⁂⁂⁂⁂⁂⁂⁂⁂⁂⁂⁂⁂⁂⁂⁂⁂⁂⁂⁂⁂

Wholesome, tender romances

YES! Please send me 2 FREE Harlequin® Heartwarming Larger-Print novels and my 2 FREE mystery gifts (gifts worth about $10). After receiving them, if I don't wish to receive any more books, I can return the shipping statement marked "cancel." If I don't cancel, I will receive 4 brand-new larger-print novels every month and be billed just $4.99 per book in the U.S. or $5.74 per book in Canada. That's a savings of at least 23% off the cover price. It's quite a bargain! Shipping and handling is just 50¢ per book in the U.S. and 75¢ per book in Canada.* I understand that accepting the 2 free books and gifts places me under no obligation to buy anything. I can always return a shipment and cancel at any time. Even if I never buy another book, the two free books and gifts are mine to keep forever.

161/361 IDN F47N

Name	(PLEASE PRINT)	
Address		Apt. #
City	State/Prov.	Zip/Postal Code

Signature (if under 18, a parent or guardian must sign)

Mail to the Harlequin® Reader Service:
IN U.S.A.: P.O. Box 1867, Buffalo, NY 14240-1867
IN CANADA: P.O. Box 609, Fort Erie, Ontario L2A 5X3

* Terms and prices subject to change without notice. Prices do not include applicable taxes. Sales tax applicable in N.Y. Canadian residents will be charged applicable taxes. Offer not valid in Quebec. This offer is limited to one order per household. Not valid for current subscribers to Harlequin Heartwarming larger-print books. All orders subject to credit approval. Credit or debit balances in a customer's account(s) may be offset by any other outstanding balance owed by or to the customer. Please allow 4 to 6 weeks for delivery. Offer available while quantities last.

Your Privacy—The Harlequin® Reader Service is committed to protecting your privacy. Our Privacy Policy is available online at www.ReaderService.com or upon request from the Harlequin Reader Service.

We make a portion of our mailing list available to reputable third parties that offer products we believe may interest you. If you prefer that we not exchange your name with third parties, or if you wish to clarify or modify your communication preferences, please visit us at www.ReaderService.com/consumerschoice or write to us at Harlequin Reader Service Preference Service, P.O. Box 9062, Buffalo, NY 14269. Include your complete name and address.

HWDIR13R

ReaderService.com

Manage your account online!

- Review your order history
- Manage your payments
- Update your address

---

*We've designed
the Harlequin® Reader Service
website just for you.*

Enjoy all the features!

- Reader excerpts from any series
- Respond to mailings and
  special monthly offers
- Discover new series available to you
- Browse the Bonus Bucks catalog
- Share your feedback

Visit us at:
ReaderService.com